"Picture it, Mr. Benson: An unscrupulous gang leader feeds these pills to half a dozen gunmen and turns them loose on a bank or payroll holdup. Insensitive to pain, so that they must be wounded mortally to be stopped, they charge ahead, savagely murdering anyone who gets in their way. And, at the same time, screaming with laughter. Horrible! Or picture an entire army treated the same way, laughing maniacally as they advance on the enemy, living only to kill, not feeling wounds, like machine men from Mars."

"We'll do what we can," the Avenger replied, and his steel-strong fingers pressed a button to begin the deadly serious pursuit of **THE HAPPY KILLERS.**

Books In This Series

By Kenneth Robeson

Published By

WARNER PAPERBACK LIBRARY

THE HAPPY KILLERS

by Kenneth Robeson

WARNER
PAPERBACK
LIBRARY

A Warner Communications Company

WARNER PAPERBACK LIBRARY EDITION
First Printing: February, 1974

This Warner Paperback Library Edition is published by
arrangement with The Condé Nast Publications, Inc.

Cover illustration by George Gross

**Warner Paperback Library is a division of Warner Books, Inc.,
75 Rockefeller Plaza, New York, N.Y. 10019.**

 A Warner Communications Company

CHAPTER I

The man with the broken nose was plainly the leader of the gang.

There were four of them, besides the man with the twisted nose, and you wouldn't have wanted to meet any one of the four in a back alley on a dark night.

One of them was a small fellow with wispy gray hair, although he couldn't have been more than thirty years old. He had dead-black eyes and practically no mouth and chin, and fingers stained a deep yellow with nicotine. Another was a stocky man with a broad scar spiraling down from his right ear to the back of his neck, about where a collar button would be. The third was immensely tall and very thin and kept twitching his forefinger as if it were tightening around a trigger. For this trait, indeed, he was called Trigger. The fourth man was a fat fellow with baby-pink lips drawn down at the left corner in a perpetual sneer.

And then, of course, there was the man with the broken

nose—big, brawny, with sand-yellow hair and muddy-gray eyes.

It was as nice a little bunch of cutthroats as you could find in New York, and they were about to get into action. And right after that all hell was going to pop. Though even the gang didn't know that at the moment.

The four were waiting beside their car, a dark sedan that could hardly be seen in the blackness of the night. It was about midnight, and cloudy. The car was on a small, curving residential street in Great Neck, Long Island. It was a dead-end street, and the sedan was near its terminus, so no other cars went by.

The man with the broken nose looked at the luminous dial of his wrist watch.

"Ten to twelve," he growled. "She oughta be here by now. Old Brown goes to bed at the tick of eleven every night, she said. He's had plenty of time to get to sleep."

The man with the twisting scar stirred uneasily.

"I don't trust that dame," he said. "How do we know—"

"Shut it! Here she is!"

There was a faint click as the iron gate in the fence surrounding the last house on the street was pressed furtively shut. A figure glided along the walk, keeping close to the hedge so that it blended in shadows. It approached the car.

"O.K.?" the leader of the murderous little gang said, softly.

"O.K.," was the return whisper.

As the figure drew closer you could see that it was a girl. The curves were there, very nice ones, and a long bob of cloudy dark hair. All feminine. But you couldn't see her face. She had on a low-brimmed hat, a mannish kind of hat, and this was arranged so that no features showed.

"The old guy pounding his ear?" said the man with the broken nose.

"Yes," whispered the girl.

"Did you get the dope?"

"Yes," the girl said again. Her voice was attractive. "I looked through the keyhole, like you said. I used the glass. I could see the numbers plainly with it."

The man grunted. "Sure. Swell little spyglass. Gimme!"

A scrap of paper passed from the girl's hand to his.

"Why didn't you get in touch with me sooner?" complained the man.

"It wasn't till tonight that he opened his safe," the girl replied. "Sometimes he goes for days without putting anything in or taking anything out. I told you that before."

"You going back to the house now?" asked the man.

The girl shook her head. "I said good-bye at ten. I'm supposed to be out till late. Then I hid, so I could leave the house door, and the gate back there, on the latch when I sneaked out. I'll keep on going now, and get back about one o'clock and be very surprised when—something has happened."

The man with the broken nose chuckled. It was not a pleasant sound.

"You're smart enough, kid. I could use you permanently if you weren't so high-hat. You'll get plenty out of this little job, though."

"See that you don't forget that," the girl said coolly. "Good-bye."

She went on down the street, keeping in shadow. There was a station on the main line about a mile and a half down. She was heading toward the depot, still keeping her head down.

"She sure is careful," said the little man with the wispy gray hair. "Who is she, anyway?"

"You wouldn't care to know," said the man with the broken nose. "Come on. Let's get going."

They walked silently to the gate, found it not quite latched, as the girl had promised, and slid into the grounds. The grounds were quite elaborate; it was apparent that a very wealthy man lived there.

The fat fellow with the babyish lips nodded enthusiastically.

"This ought to be good," he whispered. "Any servants?"

"Over the garage," he said. "Nobody'll get in our hair. It's the first room on the left when you get inside. A kind of library. You pull out a shelf, books and all, and the safe's behind it."

They went to the door like four shadows, men whose business—which they'd learned well—was to move without noise in the night. They opened the door and stepped into a dark hall.

They started toward a double doorway off the hall— and then froze. They held their breaths to listen.

There was a faint creaking sound from the stairs.

The man with the scar moved his arm slowly. It was like the slow coiling of a deadly snake. The reason for the slowness was perfectly logical: he was trying to keep the fabric of his coat from rustling.

His hand closed on the gun in his shoulder holster and drew it out. The creak sounded again from the stairs, and then a tense voice: "Who's there?"

The jaw of the man with the twisted nose tightened in anger. He'd been led to believe that there was no one in the house who would interfere.

"I saw you come in the door," came the tense voice again. "Put your hands up."

But there was lack of conviction in the unseen speaker's tone, so the four men crouched where they were, near the front door, in darkness. The creak of steps sounded as the man came nearer.

He didn't say any more and his steps hastened toward the end and became carelessly loud. The steps told the whole story to men like the crouching four. The servant—butler, house man, whatever he might be—had thought he saw movement. But he was not sure. When there was no answering noise to his hail, he believed he'd been mistaken.

He was walking quite openly when he got to the front door, and he could be seen quite plainly in the faint light coming through the glass upper panel. He reached for the doorknob to make sure the lock was on.

The man with the drawn gun swung, and swung hard. There was a sickening crunch at the end of the swing, and the fellow who had been reaching for the knob fell to the floor and did not move. He would never move again.

The man with the scar put his gun back in its holster. He straightened up so that he could be seen in the light from the panel. He spat into the palm of his right hand and pounded it with his left.

"Bad luck to bump a guy," he explained briefly. "That takes the edge off."

"It's only bad luck if you get nailed for it," the man with the twisted nose said coldly. "Did you have to sock him so hard?"

The one with the scar shrugged. "Why not? Say! I thought you said the servants slept over the garage. What's this guy doing in the house?"

"How do I know? Maybe he came in for a glass of water. Anyhow, he won't bother us now."

As if the leader had cracked some marvelously funny joke, someone laughed in the house.

It was startling. It was, with the dead man lying there

at their feet, a grisly, eerie sound. The laughter mounted, as if murder was a most comical thing.

The tall, skinny man, Trigger, grasped the nearest arm.

"*Now* what?" he rasped. "Say, I want to get outta here!"

"Keep your shirt on." The man with the twisted nose went to the library doorway. "The dame told me about that. Brown's got some nut here he's boarding. A sort of second cousin, or something. The guy goes around laughing all the time."

The weird laughter rose again, from somewhere upstairs. The man with the gray hair shivered and hunched-in his chest.

"Won't he wake up old Brown?" he quavered. "We don't want to knock off a big shot like *him*."

"Brown won't wake up," said the leader. "He's used to this bird's cackling."

He was working at a certain section of the book-lined wall as he spoke. There were hundreds of books in the place. This one section, at the right touch, swung smoothly open and revealed what the four wanted to see:

A large wall safe set solidly into the special wall behind the books.

"Boy, she's a honey," breathed the man with the scar.

"You said it, Nick," Trigger whispered back. "We'd never crack that can without enough soup to sound off from here to Times Square. Lucky that Nailen's got the combination."

The man with the twisted nose, referred to as Nailen, paid no attention to the whispers. He was whirling the knob according to the figures the girl had given him. The figures she'd spotted with the aid of a small glass through the keyhole when the owner of the house had opened his safe.

There was a smooth click, and the ponderous little door swung open. Nailen pulled a sack from under his belt.

He didn't take time to pick and choose. He simply emptied the contents of the vault into the sack—packages of money, boxes that held jewelry or other small valuables, papers, stocks and bonds, whatever was in the thing.

His eyes glinted as he did so. There was a lot of cash here. They had known there would be, or they wouldn't have taken on this job in the first place. And there was a lot of jewelry; old Brown kept all his dead wife's jewels out of sentiment.

The papers, Nailen didn't know anything about. He just took them to make a clean sweep.

The sack bulged when he was done. He clicked the safe door shut again, wiped the knob with his handkerchief, and nodded to the others. They filed toward the front door.

It was very dark in the hall. Too dark to see anything. Trigger almost fell over something soft, yet firm. His startled oath snapped out in something more than a whisper.

It was the dead man's arm that had nearly sent him sprawling.

"Ho-ho-ho!" came the laughter from upstairs. "Ha-ha-ha-ha!"

"Let's get *outta* here!" whispered the one called Nick, with a hysterical note in his voice.

They fled, with the cackling laughter pursuing them.

CHAPTER II

Death Unleashed

The street was only a short block in length, near Greenwich Village, in Manhattan.

The north side of the short block was entirely taken up by the windowless wall of an immense storage building. The south side had three narrow red-brick buildings in the center, with small warehouses and stores on each side. All the buildings on the south side were owned or leased by Richard Benson, better known as The Avenger, so that, in effect, he owned the block.

Benson's headquarters were in those three shabby-appearing buildings that looked so desolate and unkempt from the outside. Over the middle doorway was the small sign, "Justice, Inc." The other two doors were bricked-up because, inside, the three buildings had been thrown into one. A quite palatial one.

On the morning after four men had stolen into the rich home at Great Neck, a man in late middle age got out of a cab at the entrance of the little street. He paid the driver, waited till the cab had swung up the street out of sight, then glanced at the street sign and nodded. Bleeker Street, it said. That was the street he wanted.

He went toward the shabby doorway over which gently swung the inconspicuous sign, "Justice, Inc." As he walked he kept looking around to see if he were being observed. When he got to the doorway he almost ran in, as if fearing a bullet out of nowhere.

The vestibule of the building was perfectly plain, stone-lined, with one bell in the east wall. The man pressed the bell.

There was a hesitation, then the inner door swung open. The man jumped, and stared to see who had opened it. No one had. It was apparent that some hidden mechanism had swung it back for him, after some other hidden mechanism had examined him.

He went up a flight of stairs. A small frosted-glass panel glowed, with letters in its center. "Another flight up, please."

He obeyed the command jerkily, staring around, nervous as a cat. At the top of the second flight a door opened noiselessly. "Come in," said a vibrant voice.

The entire top floor of the converted building had been made into one vast room, and it was this room which was the real headquarters of Justice, Inc. The richness of the room's furnishings was an indication of the wealth the band had at its command—a wealth that was incalculable.

Near one of the windows was a great desk with a battery of telephones on it, such as might be found on the desk of a big-business executive. Behind the desk was Dick Benson.

People viewing The Avenger for the first time were always struck by two things. One was his youth. This man who was known to nearly every law-enforcing officer in the United States, and to all the police heads of the world, who was hated and feared so by the underworld that any one of a thousand big-time criminals would have given all they owned to be able to kill him, was still in his twenties.

The other noticeable factor about The Avenger was the immobility of his face. His features were regular and powerful and, as many women had noticed, quite good-looking. But they were as motionless, as expressionless, as a mask.

In this expressionlessness, his eyes, pale and clear and cold as ice, peered out with an inhuman calm. When you stared into them you could believe the incredible accounts of what The Avenger had done, in spite of his youth.

Benson looked coolly at the middle-aged man who had come to see him. The man had white hair over a smooth pink face, and was heavyset. He was dressed in good clothes, but looked as if he'd thrown them on in a hurry, or else had slept in them all night.

"Mr. Benson?" he said, with agitation in his voice. The Avenger nodded.

"My name is Brown," said the heavyset man. "Dillingham Brown."

His eyes left the compelling, pale stare of Benson's light orbs, and centered on The Avenger's head, where the thick, coal-black hair grew close and virile.

"I . . . I was robbed last night," said Brown.

Dick nodded again. "I know."

Brown was startled out of his next intended sentence. "You know? The papers don't have it yet. Nobody knows but the police—"

Benson nodded toward a far corner of the great room. Brown turned to look, and then comprehended. In the slight silence after his words, a faint clicking sounded out from the corner.

There was a teletype there, and over it flowed, day and

night, all the news of all the crime worth mentioning in the United States. What the police got, Benson got— which was fair enough. The Avenger worked with the police, was known to and respected by the police; and they were only too glad to have him know what they knew.

"Announcement of the robbery at your house in Great Neck last night came in about one o'clock," Dick said. "But from the nature of the announcement, I hardly expected to see you or have anything to do with the case."

"Why not?" said Brown, looking anxious. "I understand you always helped anyone who needed it."

The Avenger didn't answer directly. "What was taken from your wall safe?" he asked.

Brown became more agitated than before.

"The thieves got a tremendous haul," he said. "There was nearly a hundred thousand dollars' worth of jewelry, conservatively estimated. My wife's things, kept by me since she died. There was about the same amount in cash." Brown looked a bit embarrassed. "Times are so uncertain," he mumbled. "Good idea to have some money at hand, outside of banks. And there were stocks and bonds, papers that I can't replace—books on trust funds which I administer, some accounts of stocks and bond transfers for clients— It was a great blow to me."

"Exactly," said The Avenger, patiently.

"Eh?" said Brown, looking bewildered. "Exactly what? How do you mean, 'exactly'?"

"You suffered a large but quite ordinary loss. Jewelry, money, financial papers. That is not in my province, Mr. Brown."

The Avenger leaned back at his huge desk.

"Justice, Inc.," he said, "is in existence to help people who are in trouble of a nature which prevents the police from assisting them. Crime of a nature so fantastic that

16

the police are unequipped to handle it, persecution of a type that is above the law, rather than beyond it—these are the things we take on. But your case is just ordinary robbery. The police are the ones to handle that."

"But the police are already working on it," protested Brown. "And they're getting nowhere."

"Sorry," Dick said politely. "We don't mix into routine police jobs."

"Then you won't—" Brown began, looking crushed with disappointment.

He stopped. Then he came forward as if very tired and sat in the chair beside The Avenger's desk. He slumped into it and put his head in his hands.

"There was more taken than mere valuables," he said in a different tone. "Something among the papers the thieves got when they emptied the safe—"

He looked up at Benson in a defeated, terrified way.

"I didn't tell the police about it. I didn't want to tell even you about it. I just hoped the loot would be recovered and the thing would be there with the rest of it, and I'd never have to say a word. The contents of my safe must be recovered, Mr. Benson. Because among the papers there is a . . . a chemical formula that is a dreadful thing."

He lowered his voice to a whisper, as if fearing that the very walls would listen and repeat the story.

"It's for a drug that turns a man into a laughing killer!"

The Avenger's face remained as masklike as before. The pale and icy eyes were as inhumanly calm. But their colorless glitter increased till they were like diamond probes.

Brown went on. "The money and jewelry—forget them. The private account books of the trust funds I administer —the loss is serious but not ruinous. But that drug—" He shuddered, as if very ill.

"Just what is the drug?" asked Benson.

"It's a form of laughing gas. That's as near as I can describe it. A young cousin of mine, Harry Tate, invented it. The boy is living with me. I put him through school. Years ago he got the idea that if some anaesthetic could be discovered that could be administered orally, in pill form, it would be a wonderful thing on a battlefield. No complicated apparatus such as is now needed, no sterilizing equipment for the use of local anaesthetics; just take a wounded man, have him swallow a pill, and then operate painlessly.

"Harry has worked on that idea for a long time. He tried it with ether and chloroform compounds, and got nowhere. Then he began experimenting with ordinary laughing gas, in use in most dentists' offices. His work and experiments backfired. Instead of coming up with a harmless anaesthetic to be administered quickly and easily in pill form, he got a monstrous kind of drug that could turn life in this country into a nightmare if some underworld leader got hold of it. Or it could change the course of history if foreign dictators found it out."

Brown put his head in his hands again and moaned.

"Harry stumbled onto a concoction that makes a person insensible to pain but does not anaesthetize. That is, the conscious will, the power to move around and think and act, is untouched. You could be stabbed or shot and not know it till you fell over, later, for lack of blood. But worse, the drug stimulates the savage instincts in some way that even Harry can't explain, so that it turns a normally peaceful person into a raging killer. A killer who *laughs!*"

"Laughs?" said The Avenger.

"Yes. Remember, the base of this formula is similar in character to the ordinary laughing gas that dentists use. Anyone taking it suffers from the same symptom—helpless, prolonged laughter. At the same time, he is stirred to murderous rage against almost every moving thing he sees."

Brown drew a long, ragged breath.

"Picture it, Mr. Benson: An unscrupulous gang leader feeds these pills to half a dozen gunmen and turns them loose on a bank or payroll holdup. Insensitive to pain, so that they must be wounded mortally to be stopped, they charge ahead, savagely murdering anyone who gets in their way. And, at the same time, screaming with laughter. Horrible! Or picture an entire army treated the same way, laughing maniacally as they advance on the enemy, living only to kill, not feeling wounds, like machine men from Mars."

There followed a silence in which the purr of the teletype in the far corner seemed loud. Then The Avenger said evenly, "You don't know any more of the composition of this formula than you have told me?"

"No," sighed Brown. "I'd tell you if I knew. But I don't know. I've seen what the pills can do. Harry warned me of the tremendous importance of the formula in its present uncompleted state. That's all I know."

He looked pleadingly at The Avenger.

"But you see why this is no ordinary theft? You see why every effort must be made to get the papers from my safe back before the formula is discovered for what it is? My only hope is that it can be recovered without even the police seeing it. Otherwise, the secret might leak out."

The slim but steel-strong finger of The Avenger pressed a buzzer on his desk.

"We'll do what we can," he said.

CHAPTER III

Murder—Without Motive!

A secondary headquarters for Justice, Inc., was the drugstore of Fergus MacMurdie, not far from Bleeker Street. The store looked like any other drugstore from the front. There were the standard counters with the standard contents. There was the usual soda fountain. But the back room of the store was twice as large as the front, and it was not at all standard.

Each half was a beautifully equipped laboratory. One half went in for electrical and radio apparatus of all sorts. The other half was a chemist's paradise.

Fergus MacMurdie, nominal proprietor of the store, was the chemist concerned. Few in the world could equal his ability; and many weird concoctions had been turned out in his test tubes and beakers. The other half of the big room belonged to Smitty, electrical wizard, who was another member of The Avenger's band.

Mac was in the front of the store with Cole Wilson, Justice, Inc.'s newest member, at about the time Dillingham Brown was talking to Dick Benson on Bleeker Street. It was too bad that MacMurdie and Wilson couldn't have overheard that talk; they would not have been so unprepared for what was about to happen to them.

"Ye'll drive me into bankruptcy," Mac was saying to Cole. "Josh comes in and laps up maple-nut sundaes—on the house. Ye come in and fill your pockets with candy—on the house. Ye're a bunch of deadheads."

Mac was very tall, and very sandy of hair and eyebrows, very homely and very Scotch. He had coarse reddish skin with great freckles just underneath the surface. But one look into his frosty, bleak blue eyes and you didn't laugh at his appearance.

"Trouble with you," retorted Cole Wilson equably, "is that you'd rather lose your right arm than a nickel."

Cole was as handsome as Mac was homely. Cole had dark thick hair which he never covered with a hat, and had an Indian straightness of feature and litheness of body. He was a good man to have beside you in a fight.

"Trouble with you," he went on, "is that you pinch every penny till Lincoln thinks it's the Civil War all over again."

"Is that so?" snapped Mac. "If ye'd stop spendin' all ye get yer hands on, ye'd maybe have a little put by for yer old age. Like me."

Cole laughed. "Go on. None of us will have an old age. You know that. Working for a boss like The Avenger doesn't tend to make you live long!"

This was so true that the bony Scot was stuck for a further retort. But even if he'd thought of one, he wouldn't have had time to make it. For it was then that the curious thing occurred. Curious? No, that's a mild word. It was a mad thing; a crazed, frightening, incredible thing.

Looking through the show window, Mac saw a man on the sidewalk who seemed to have just heard the world's funniest joke. He was laughing so that tears were streaming down his face. He was hooting with laughter so that everyone in earshot was turning to look, and it could even be heard, a little, inside the store.

Mac scratched his sandy thatch, interested but not warned in any way. "Where'd the mon come from?" he wondered aloud. "I didn't see him walk up."

The reason for that was that the laughing man had just stepped out of a car, which had paused at the curb and then darted off instantly. Mac hadn't been watching the street closely enough to see the car, so the effect was as if the man had suddenly appeared out of nowhere.

Cole watched the fellow and grinned a little in sympathy.

"He must have seen or heard something screamingly funny in the last couple of minutes."

Mac, looking harder now, shook his head. Mac was an accredited physician as well as a foremost pharmacist. His eye took on the glint of a diagnostician's.

" 'Tis not norrmal laughter," burred the Scot. "Somethin' ails the mon—"

"Looks like he's coming in here," Cole interrupted.

The man, still laughing so that he was crying, started for the drugstore door. As he opened it his wild laughter hit full on the eardrums of Mac and Cole. And it didn't sound at all funny.

"Ha-ha-ha!" laughed the man, staring, with eyes that were distinctly unhumorous, at the two men. "Ho-ho!"

Laughing, he drew a gun!

"Watch him!" yelled Cole. *"Duck!"*

The warning was unnecessary. Completely bewildered, but seeing death in the man's eyes and reacting with the instant efficiency that all of The Avenger's aides displayed in time of peril, Mac was on the floor behind the soda fountain.

"Ho-ho-ho. Hee-hee," laughed the man with the gun.

He leaned over the fountain and fired twice at Mac's fleeing shape.

It was weird, uncanny! Quite apart from the real danger of flying lead, it sent shivers of fear up and down Mac's spine. The shouts of laughter, as if at some exquisite joke. The ripples and waves of mirth. And in the midst of this—eyes that were crazed with the urge to murder!

"Ho-ho-ho," roared the man, shooting into the end counter, behind which Mac had crawled.

Cole acted then from the opposite side of the room. He picked up the first thing at hand on a counter, and threw it. It was a pint-size, cheap vacuum bottle. It hit the laughing murderer squarely on the temple, broke, and sliced a deep gash there.

Again the ripple of supernatural fear ran down their spines. It was a nasty gash; it should have been very painful. But the laughing gunman didn't even seem to know he'd been cut. He choked with laughter and sent two more slugs into the counter that hid the Scot. Then he whirled toward Cole.

He was a little late with this move. Cole was already in mid-air, leaping like a giant cat for the man. A slug almost parted his thick dark hair for him; then the man was down, banging his head against the floor so that it sounded like a dropped melon.

Even this didn't seem to faze him. The man laughed as if it were the funniest thing that had happened yet and looped a savage right toward Wilson's face. Cole barely managed to get out of the way of the blow and slammed a fist against the man's jaw.

It rocked the fellow's head till it looked as if his neck were broken. It should have knocked out a heavyweight champion. But this fellow, undersized if anything, and not looking at all strong, kept right on hitting back.

"What in the worrld!" burred Mac, staring.

"Gas him!" gasped Wilson, struggling to keep from being thrown off. "Do something!"

"Watch ye'rsel'," was Mac's response.

The Scot tossed something that looked like a little silver pill.

It was a glass pellet with an anaesthetic gas of his own devising that would knock out a horse in about three seconds. Cole buried his nose in the lapel of his coat, chemically treated to act as an impromptu mask against the gas. He breathed through this as the laughing man inhaled the gas from the broken pellet and promptly slipped into unconsciousness. And there was a shattered silence in the store.

Cole got up from the limp figure and looked dazedly at Mac, who shook his head to express his own bewilderment.

"A mon comes in here cold, laughin' like a loon—and tries to murrder us," the Scot burred. "It just doesn't make sense."

"Either a lunatic or all hopped up," was Cole's verdict. "Probably the latter. He looks like a professional gunman."

They examined the prone figure. The man was undersized and ratlike, with cheap flashy clothes and the soft, uncalloused hands of one who does not toil for a living. Mac took his pulse and found it rapid and steady. He lifted the eyelids and stared into pupil-contracted eyes.

"Some sort of drug," he nodded. "But I wonder what the joke was that made him laugh so much."

"Let's take him to the back room, wait till he comes to, and find out," suggested Cole. "We'll—"

He lifted his head and listened intently. A soft buzzing sound was coming from the back room in question.

"The boss wants us," he said. "That's the television buzzer. Bleeker Street's calling."

Mac nodded. "You take care of our laughing friend, Cole. I'll see what's up."

At the end of the big back room was a large case containing the world's finest television set. An invention of Smitty's, it beat the finest commercial products by far. Normally, it was kept tuned to the Bleeker Street sender; and when The Avenger wanted someone in Mac's drugstore, that little buzzer sounded.

The screen on the front of the cabinet was glowing as Mac walked up to it.

"Go ahead, Muster Benson," the Scot said into the transmitter.

But it was not the immobile countenance and pale, deadly eyes of The Avenger that showed. In the screen appeared the good-natured face of Smitty; and in Smitty's face was an excitement to match Mac's own.

Smitty's full name was Algernon Heathcote Smith, but only close friends could call him that without getting mauled. And no one in his right mind would risk getting mauled by Smitty. He was six feet nine, weighed close to three hundred pounds, all of it bone and brawn, and had a chest so bulging that his arms couldn't hang down straight. He had innocent blue eyes and a good-humored face. And he was dynamite on legs!

Smitty's usual companion was a small and dainty person who made such contrast with his giant size that passers-by snickered to see them together. This was Nellie Gray, a valuable aid of The Avenger. Nellie was barely five feet tall, barely a hundred pounds heavy, and looked as if an unkind word would make her cry for an hour. Actually she could throw grown men around with her jujitsu and wrestling tricks, and could shoot and box like a marine.

She and Smitty had been on the second floor of the Bleeker Street place when Benson rang for them, after Brown had had his talk. They came up fast, sensing a fight. Both of them lived for the battles with the underworld that made Justice, Inc. so feared. Nellie's gentle, dreamy-eyed, archaeologist father had been murdered by crooks after secret treasure which he knew about. Smitty had once been framed into prison by a suave criminal. Hence, both burned with a permanent revenge and were never completely happy unless they were making some human rat regret that he'd been born.

The pale glint in The Avenger's icy eyes told them something was up, all right.

Benson sketched what Brown had told him.

"Let me get it straight," said the giant Smitty, at the conclusion. He frowned incredulously. "You mean somebody named Harry Tate has cooked up a stew that makes a man want to go out and murder somebody? And laugh while he does it?"

"That's approximately right," said Benson. Even Smitty and Nellie couldn't read the thought behind his motionless features.

"That's pretty hard to swallow," Nellie objected. "What kind of stuff could do that?"

"Brown said it was a concentrated form of laughing gas. It was intended to take the place of a standard anaesthetic, to be administered in pill form. But instead of rendering the subject unconscious, it merely makes him insensitive to pain. And also, in some fashion, it stirs up all his murderous instincts."

"So if you gave somebody one of those pills," said Smitty, "and then commanded him to go out and murder someone, he'd do it—and laugh while he did it. Wow! That's no kind of pill to have in the hands of a bunch of crooks."

"If there is such a pill," said little Nellie.

The Avenger nodded toward the big television cabinet which matched the one in Mac's drugstore. "I think Wilson and Mac are at the store," he said. "Contact them, Smitty, and get them over here."

"I still say it's impossible," the little blond said stubbornly. "There isn't any such—"

Then Smitty got his reply from Mac. The Scot's bony features showed on the screen. And, as if in direct answer to Nellie's doubts, Mac blurted out:

"Say! We just had a queerrr and unnatural occurrence. A mon came into the drugstore, laughin' like he was about to bust, and tried to murder Wilson and me."

"What?" cried Nellie.

Smitty gaped at the reflection of Mac's homely mug. The Avenger said nothing; he simply stared with eyes like pale jewels in their brilliance.

"Didn't ye hear me?" snapped Mac peevishly. "I said a mon seemed to think it was a great joke to kill Cole and me."

The Avenger spoke from the desk. "Did you get him, Mac?"

"Yes, Muster Benson. Cole has him in the front of the store. Wait a minute."

Smitty and Benson and Nellie could hear a faint howl; Cole Wilson's voice. Then Mac came scowling back to the screen.

"We *did* have the mon, Muster Benson," he said sourly. "But it seems he got Cole off guard, swatted him with an electric toaster, and got away. We thought he was out for an hour, but ye see, nothin' seemed to hurt him. It was as if he couldn't feel pain like normal folks."

"Holy mackerel!" breathed Smitty. "It's true then!"

The Avenger said evenly, "Better come over here right away. We'll look into this at once."

CHAPTER IV

Edna Brown

All of the members of Justice, Inc. faced one another in the vast top-floor room on Bleeker Street—Cole Wilson and MacMurdie, Smitty and Nellie, The Avenger himself, and Josh and Rosabel Newton.

These latter two were as effective as any other of the band, though they didn't look it. Josh was a tall, gangling Negro who constantly looked as if he were about to go to sleep on his huge feet. Actually, he was an honor graduate of Tuskegee Institute, and had a brain like a steel trap. His occasional lapses into a deep drawl, and his sleepy look, were deliberately cultivated to make folks think he was duller than he was. Rosabel, his wife, was a pretty Negro woman with liquid dark eyes, a gentle manner and a will of iron. She had saved more than one of Dick Benson's hard-living crew from death.

The Avenger had just told MacMurdie the reason, as it seemed, at least, for the crazy, unprovoked attack by the man in the drugstore. The others had all listened, popeyed. And Mac was as incredulous as Nellie had been over the existence of such a drug.

But the laughing killer's insane entrance into his store was proof enough, even for him.

The general verdict was the same as Smitty's: The secret of such a sinister drug must not be allowed to remain in criminal hands.

The way to retrieve the formula, of course, was to recover the contents of Brown's safe. Which meant locating the gang that had looted it.

"Josh, Rosabel," The Avenger said, in the quiet but vibrant voice of a born leader, "you had better stay here next to the teletype and relay any possible police news of the robbery investigation to us. They'll be working hard on it. There was murder, you know—Brown's valet."

The pale, icy eyes swung to Smitty and Nellie, and then included Wilson.

"Nellie, there was talk of a woman connected with the case. The Great Neck station agent reported that a girl, whose face he couldn't see, bought a ticket to Manhattan at about midnight last night. That was the approximate time of the robbery. She might have no connection, but check on her anyway.

"Smitty, Cole, circulate around, talk to a few fences, see if there has been any attempt to dispose of the bonds or stocks from Brown's safe. Here are duplicate lists of the serial numbers."

Mac was looking as disappointed as a hurt child because he was being left out of this. But then The Avenger turned to him, and at his words the Scot's bleak eyes filled with joy.

"You and I will look over the safe and have a talk with the police, at Brown's house, Mac."

Benson and Mac went out in The Avenger's favorite car, a shabby-looking old sedan whose dingy hood was bursting with a motor that would drive them at a hundred and twenty miles an hour, if necessary. On the way, Benson summed up a little of Dillingham Brown's background.

Brown was a prominent investment counselor with a thorough legal training, specializing in the formation and handling of trust funds. Under his care were many prominent accounts, from the foundations of rich men, kept up to endow laboratories or research endeavors, to the funds left in trust for widows and orphans.

Brown, however, was chiefly known as having once been the partner of William Xenan. They'd separated about three years before; and since that time Xenan, a corporation lawyer and more recently a financier, had rocketed up into the millions and left Brown—though quite wealthy—far behind.

"What's this talk of Harry Tate?" Mac asked.

The Avenger told of the young man in Brown's house. "He has evidently been working for some years on the idea of a total anaesthetic in pill form. I've talked to the sergeant in charge at Brown's place, and he said he'd questioned Tate and thought he was a little off balance mentally. There is even a slight suspicion that Tate is the guilty party; that he stole down and robbed the safe and killed the valet."

"But why would the young mon do that?" asked Mac.

"There isn't a clear motive. He doesn't seem to be a mercenary type. Brown gave him all the money that he needed. And certainly he wouldn't have to steal his own formula from the safe. The police, by the way, have not been told of the formula. Brown begged that that be kept secret."

The police examinations of Brown's house and household had been completed by the time Mac and The Avenger arrived and there was one plainclothesman there.

That was all. He, it came out, was waiting around on the chance that Brown's maid would come back.

"Left last night about nine," said the man. "That is, Brown thought she'd left at that time. Said she wanted to visit her sister in Manhattan. But we haven't located any sister, and the station agent at the depot thinks it was the maid that left at midnight."

"The other servants?" Dick said.

The plainclothesman was looking almost in awe at Benson. He had never seen The Avenger before and could hardly believe the stories of great strength he'd heard about him. He had an idea he'd be able to break Benson in two; but he had another idea, after another look into the icy eyes, that it would not be wise to try.

"They were all out in their quarters over the garage," he said. "Each can alibi the others, so they're out. The valet, Peter Sheeley, was the only one in the house. We don't know why he was in there, at midnight. He was the one who got bumped off."

"Harry Tate?"

The plainclothesman shook his head. "Cracked, if you ask me. Want to talk to him?"

The Avenger did want to talk to him. The man got him.

Harry Tate, described by Brown as "a young cousin of mine," was about twenty-six. He was slender, slow in movement, dreamy-eyed. His every action was that of a man half out of this world, though he seemed intelligent enough.

He shook The Avenger's hand admiringly. "As a chemist," he said, "I'm familiar with some of your work. You would be the world's best-known research worker if only you didn't spend your time chasing after . . . er . . . criminals."

"Sometimes that is more valuable work than chemical

research," Benson said quietly. "You were here last night, Mr. Tate?"

Tate nodded and into his eyes came a guarded look.

"You heard nothing during the night?"

"Nothing," said Tate.

"Mr. Brown told me that he thought he heard a noise downstairs at about midnight. Then he heard you laughing. Rather, he believed it was you. Why were you laughing?"

Tate's eyes became more guarded. He glanced furtively at the plainclothesman down the hall. Evidently, the man hadn't been told about the laughter.

"I was working on a certain experiment," Tate said. "I . . . it turned out wrong, and I laughed."

"You weren't, perhaps, using yourself as an experimental subject? You didn't swallow something that made you laugh?"

Tate said nothing. He bit his lips and looked most uncomfortable.

"Won't the loss of your formula, stolen with the rest of the things from the safe, be a serious blow to you?"

Tate answered very reluctantly: "No. I . . . I can reproduce it from memory."

The Avenger saw that he'd get nothing more out of Tate, so he turned with Mac to the room of the crime. The body of the valet was at the undertaking chamber, so they could not examine it at the moment. It had told little, anyway, except that the death had been caused by a blow with a blunt instrument, probably a clubbed automatic.

The wall safe didn't tell much either.

No prints had been found on the knob; it had been carefully wiped. Someone knowing the combination had opened it, because there was no sign of violent entry. Brown's own prints were on the metal around the knob. That was all.

The house had a good burglar-alarm protection but this had been switched off by someone inside, probably that maid. The outer gate and the front door had been easily opened, so probably they had been left not quite shut by the same person, the girl—

"Hello," muttered Mac. "Who's *this* girrrl?"

Mac wasn't particularly susceptible to feminine charms, but there was a glint in his eyes as he stared at the figure that had suddenly appeared in the library doorway. Benson turned to look and saw why.

On the threshold was a girl in a maroon wool dress who could have stepped into the front line of a chorus. She was tall and slender. Her hair was ash-blond, and her eyes were light amber, like candy. She came into the room, looking at The Avenger.

"You're Mr. Benson, aren't you?" she said in a voice as charming as the rest of her. "I'm Edna Brown. I just came today to visit my father, and stepped into this mess. Isn't it dreadful?"

"Quite," The Avenger said evenly. His eyes went like drills into the amber orbs of the girl. "You say you just got here?"

"About an hour ago," she said. "I have a job in the city. Librarian. But I was down in Washington visiting a friend, during a week off, when I heard from Dad. I came up by plane."

"Oh. You thought your father had been hurt, and hurried because of that?" suggested Benson.

"No. I didn't hurry for that reason." Edna Brown looked around almost as furtively as Harry Tate had. There were only Benson and Mac and herself in the room.

"I hurried because I have an idea who might have done this," she whispered. "I haven't told the police. In fact, I don't dare tell my suspicions. As soon as I heard you were on the case, I waited to tell you."

"Good," said The Avenger, face expressionless but eyes as cold and pale as ice under a polar moon. "Who do you think it is?"

She paused for so long that it seemed she wasn't going to answer. Then she whispered, "I don't think I'd better name names, even to you. I'll do better. I'll take you to a place where I think the contents of the safe might be hidden."

The Avenger nodded. Mac was bursting with questions, but didn't ask them. The three went out to the old sedan.

CHAPTER V

False Guidance

There's a lot of length to Long Island. Far out are some pretty desolate stretches of beach, low and sandy, with a few summer cabins here and there, deserted save in mid-summer.

It was to such a section, it developed, that Edna was leading Mac and The Avenger. Meanwhile, she was being as obstinate as she was pretty—obstinate about not telling them any more than she had at first.

She had an idea that she knew who took the stuff from the safe, or caused it to be taken. But she wouldn't say who. She thought she knew where it might be hidden, but she wouldn't say how she'd come to her conclusions.

"My suspicions might be wrong," she said. "If so, and I named names, a lot of trouble could come of it."

Her stubbornness was maddening. To Mac, at least. The Avenger didn't seem to be annoyed by it. His face was as masklike, his pale eyes as unreadable as ever, when, near the very tip of the island, Edna pointed and said, "There."

The thing she was pointing at was just a speck far down the lonely road. The Avenger stopped and looked at it through a small but powerful glass.

The speck was pretty big through the glass. It was the wreck of a structure whose nature Benson guessed at a glance. It was a sort of small auditorium, in which at one time fights had no doubt been held, and which probably had a floor suitable for dancing or roller skating. The roof was half fallen in now, and boards were off the walls in spots.

It was as deserted and gloomy-looking as could be imagined.

"You think the things from your father's wall safe are hidden there?" The Avenger said evenly.

Edna nodded her ash-blond head.

"And you don't want to tell why you think so?"

She shook her head. The Avenger sent the car forward again.

The big low building was right on the water's edge, which was one reason why it was disintegrating so fast: the waves of any big storm could work on it. On the bay side, the water seemed to extend under the building. Perhaps it had been a boathouse arrangement, once. On the other side there was windswept sand from road to building where once a drive and parking lot had been. The Avenger stared at this expanse of sand, roughened in many places, and his steel-strong fingers tightened ever so slightly about the wheel.

He drove the sedan up the sand till it nosed almost against the building. He got out, and Mac noticed with a narrowing of his bleak blue eyes that The Avenger was moving with his arms held just a little from his sides, and tending to walk just a bit on the balls of his feet, like a great cat.

He walked as if he expected trouble.

If so, however, he didn't express it in words. He spoke calmly to the girl. "Where inside do you think the loot will be hidden?"

"I . . . I don't know," Edna Brown faltered. She had gone pale and was glancing nervously around. "We'll have to look."

She was next to one of the places where some boards were off, making a kind of ragged doorway into the cavernous darkness of the place. Her voice echoed inside and came faintly back: "—*have to look.*"

Benson took a powerful small flashlight from his pocket. Its cold white ray went through the ragged opening and played over a once smooth, but now weathered, floor, with supporting pillars scattered every few feet. It showed scarred walls with tattered posters of prize fights long forgotten, a pile of planks at the end that must have been set up for benches.

The three stepped inside. Far to the left there was dim light where the roof had collapsed and was open in slits to the sky. But it was quite dark and seemed ever darker because their eyes were still conscious of daylight.

Mac felt a finger touch his wrist, and felt a code in varied pressure. A message from Benson to him. It said: *"Others are here."*

Mac looked swiftly at the girl, who was only a dim blur. The Avenger would have spoken that aloud, obviously, if he hadn't wanted to keep it from Edna Brown. Therefore, he did not trust her. Mac wondered why. He couldn't imagine that the daughter of Dillingham Brown would be working against them, and hence working against her own father.

Mac's bony hand suddenly caught Benson's arm, and not in any code pressure, either.

"Did ye hear?" he whispered.

"Yes," said Benson.

It came again, the sound that had so agitated Mac. It was a laugh.

From back there in the deepest darkness, near the piled planks, it sounded. A grating, maniacal chuckle that was at once followed by a peal of laughter that echoed around the great empty auditorium as if a crowd of devils were there.

Mac began to sweat. He knew all too well the caliber of that laughter. It was the same senseless, spine-shivering sound that had come from the lips of the man who had tried to murder him and Cole at the store!

Like the call of one weird bird of prey to another, an answering laugh came from another dark corner of the place. And then there was the shuffle of footsteps. How many, they could not say.

"I'm . . . I'm going to get out of here," whispered the girl, her teeth chattering.

Benson said nothing; he allowed her to slip out through the plank opening without raising a hand to stop her. For an instant her slim body was silhouetted in the opening.

There was a fiendish laugh and the bark of a gun!

Splinters flew from the side of the opening almost under the girl's hand. She screamed and leaped out. And Mac and The Avenger whirled toward the spot where the orange lash of the gunshot had blossomed.

" 'Tis a trrap!" snapped Mac. "She led us into a tr—"

Then half a dozen more shots snapped at the sound of his voice. Several of them hit Mac, but the marvelous bulletproof stuff which Benson had invented, called celluglass, worn under his clothes, stopped the slugs.

The two of them leaped forward, weaving as they ran, heading straight toward the piled planks. That was The Avenger's way. He would walk into a trap, open-eyed, on the chance that he could learn something. If an enemy tried to ambush him, he would charge the ambush.

No telling how many were behind those planks, but it sounded like a lot; the screams of laughter might have come from a score of throats. The two men charged anyway, and when they got near, Mac tossed one of his glittering little gas pellets so that it fell between the planks and end wall.

It should have stopped things right there, but it so happened that the ambushers were on the move at that second. They poured from behind each end of the pile of boards, and fanned toward Mac and Benson. They didn't know of the knock-out mist they were leaving behind, but the move saved them as efficiently as if they had known all about it and acted accordingly.

Mac reached for another glass pellet, but the nearest man, laughing so that tears streamed down his face, reached him and began throttling him, so the Scot had to use both hands to protect himself.

He heard a slight crack beside him, a quick breath, and then heard a thundering thump to the rear. Knowledge of The Avenger's mode of fighting told him what had occurred. A man had charged Benson, had been picked up like a feather in those slight but steel-strong hands, and then had been tossed over The Avenger's shoulder to land a dozen feet behind. The crack had been either a broken arm or a terribly dislocated shoulder. Benson didn't fool when he fought. He never took a life, but he apparently held it no wrong to give a crook all the punishment he asked for.

Mac's bony fists were flailing out now like ivory mallets. There was no more shooting. Perhaps the laughing, yelling men had orders to capture the two alive. Perhaps they felt they couldn't shoot at close quarters without hitting each other. Or perhaps they were attacking with fists and clubbed guns for the malevolent pleasure of feeling the damage they were inflicting at close range.

Mac had an idea it was the latter. The baleful glitter of eyeballs, in the dim light from the roofless section, was enough to foster that idea.

Someone hit the Scot from behind like a laughing cannon ball. He went down. Mad hands felt for his throat. Maniacal laughter roared out from the owner of the hands as he found the windpipe he was after.

Mac drove his wrists up between the wrists at his neck, and shoved them wide, tearing the murderous grip loose.

"Ye skurlie," he growled, like a power saw on a muted note. "Ye would, would ye?"

He sent a left and right into the face above, felt the owner roll backward, still laughing. He got to his feet.

Off to his left, while his eyes had been near the floor level, he thought he'd seen a queer movement in the floor itself. But he didn't have time to look again, because the man he'd hit was on him again.

That was the hell of this fight, he was finding out. It was a duplicate of the eerie way the man had acted in the drugstore.

These men apparently could not be hurt. At least, they couldn't seem to be stopped, short of actually being killed. A stooped, distorted figure was cutting across behind Mac's opponent, and the Scot realized it was the man The Avenger had thrown. His shoulder was out of joint. So badly that it made you feel sick to look.

But the fellow, laughing as if he had been merely tickled, was boring in just the same, with one arm hanging slack beside him but the other groping for Benson.

Mac hit his personal assailant in the jaw so hard that it seemed to turn the man's head clear around on his neck. And the man fell at last. Unconsciousness *could* be induced, it appeared, by a blow about four times as hard as was normally necessary to knock out a man.

The Scot saw two other forms on the floor, felled by The Avenger. But there were eight or nine left on their feet, so he was too busy to see how Benson was making out.

He was too busy to see something else, too: the sequel to the queer movement he'd seen in the floor while he was sprawled there.

The movement was caused by the lifting of a section of the floor. A trapdoor, about three feet by seven, was thrown back. A head appeared; then the whole body came up. But the man didn't mix in to the fight. Instead, he went toward the opening through which Mac and Benson and the girl had come.

The girl was still out there, near the car. The figure that had emerged from the trapdoor darted out, and Edna Brown screamed.

Mac heard the scream. It sounded, a shriek of terror, over the insane laughter of men who were trying to murder them with their bare hands. There was another scream, ominously cut short.

Mac knocked out another man with a terrific sock, and turned to go to the girl's aid. Two more men caught him and tried to pull him down. He didn't see the figure from the trapdoor come back into the building, carrying the girl over his shoulder like a roll of carpet. He didn't see Edna being taken down through the trapdoor.

But The Avenger must have seen.

"Mac!" his call rang out.

Then there was a sickening thud, and he said no more. Mac didn't say any more, either, or do any more. Because at about the same time a blow from a club or something at last caught him squarely. It was as if the roof had fallen on his skull.

Mac was not quite out. From a far distance he heard

the cackling, maniacal laughter. Faintly he felt something being done to his ankles and wrists. Then he heard a roar, seemingly from right underneath him. The roar was swiftly muted and then there was silence.

The silence, after a while, with his wits returning, was broken just a little by a curious crackling noise.

Mac stirred on the floor and sat up. He did this with difficulty, because his hands and feet were bound; it was the tightening of ropes he'd felt faintly a moment ago at wrists and ankles.

He looked around. To his left was a figure that, in a moment, he recognized as Dick Benson's. The others lying around had been carried off.

He wondered for a minute why he could see Dick so clearly in this darkness. Then he realized that there was a little light that hadn't existed before. And he realized the light was reddish and unsteady.

"Muster Benson!" he yelled. "Chief!"

The place had been fired. Tongues of flame were beginning to catch all around them.

Benson stirred. Mac inwardly thanked heaven for that, although he should have known that The Avenger was not dead, as he had feared at first. Veteran fighters such as these two can almost always half-see, or sense, a head blow coming and can roll with it so that they receive minimum damage. Dick had done this, obviously, even as Mac had, with the result that they were knocked out for a minute but not killed.

The Avenger snapped to consciousness in almost the same way he habitually awakened—with all his senses alert and full comprehension of what had just gone on. A glance of the pale eyes at the ring of flame, a tentative move to reveal bonds at feet and hands, and The Avenger was in action.

All Benson's clothes were specially made, with scores of tiny pockets all over them in which were tiny weapons, chemicals, gadgets of a dozen kinds useful in attack, defense or escape. In this case, escape.

Mac saw Benson's little shoulders move, and then saw a glitter as The Avenger's bound hands worked his left trouser leg up. The glitter was caused by Ike.

Dick Benson habitually went armed only with two small and unimpressive-looking weapons. One was a small .22 revolver of his own design, equipped with a special silencer, and which he called, in grim affection, "Mike." The other was a slender throwing knife with a hollow tube for a handle, which he called "Ike."

He wore Mike in a narrow holster at his right calf, and Ike in a sheath at his left. Since captors seldom bother to search men below the knees, these two sleek little weapons were seldom discovered.

They hadn't been discovered this time, either. And it was Ike that The Avenger was working to get. His supple fingers closed over the razor-keen blade, and he crawled to where Mac was. He pressed the knife against Mac's bonds, and a moment later was free himself.

"So we were left to toast!" Mac rapped out. "The murderin skur—"

The Avenger didn't waste time on recriminations. He leaped to the plank opening and out. There was nothing in sight down the road. He ran to the beach side of the building, stared out toward the mainland shore, then whipped out the small telescope.

"Power boat," he said to Mac, voice as calm as if he had not just been condemned to burn to death. "They got away in a boat."

It told Mac the source of the roar he'd heard underneath him while his senses had been swimming from that blow. There still was a boathouse arrangement under the building, then. And a fast boat had been concealed there for a getaway.

"They've got the girl with them," Dick said, looking through the glass.

"Why not?" snarled Mac. "She was one of them. Didn't she lead us right into their hands? Take us to where her father's valuables were hidden, huh!"

But even as he spoke, the Scot knew he was off the track somewhere. If the girl had been in with this crew, why had she screamed in such deadly fear when she was confronted by one of them?

They were yards from the building, but the heat of its burning made them uncomfortable. They hurried to the opposite side, where the car was. The slight wind was blowing away from this side, fortunately. At the expense of singed eyebrows, they rolled the sedan back out of danger. It wasn't long after that when the building fell in, a mass of flaming embers.

The Avenger started rolling down the road away from it, a calm, enigmatic figure over the steering wheel.

"I don't get it," Mac repeated helplessly. "She *couldn't* be in with the gang that robbed her father. Yet, she turned us over to them. And it must be the same gang because of the laughin'. They've already started to use Tate's drug to make them brave and immune to pain."

Dick said nothing.

Mac went on: "Say! Maybe it wasn't any maid that let the gang into Brown's house last night. Maybe it was Brown's own daughter."

Benson said nothing.

"Ye can see now why she wouldn't tell us anythin'," Mac said experimentally, looking sideways at the immobile face. "She couldn't, without givin' her own crooked partners away."

Still, The Avenger said nothing, so Mac gave it up. When the man with the colorless, terrible eyes didn't choose to talk, no power on earth could make him.

CHAPTER VI

Cold Trail

It was about dusk, with Manhattan's towers not far ahead, when the car radio broke in on Mac's perplexed thoughts. The radio was tuned to Justice, Inc.'s own private wave band. The voice of Cole Wilson sounded.

"No sign anywhere of Brown's stocks and bonds. Maybe the crooks are going to wait awhile before trying to dispose of them. Maybe they're too smart to do anything with them at all."

Wilson's voice snapped off, and the big, shabby-looking sedan rolled on in more silence. Then Mac tried again. He couldn't get answers from The Avenger on important questions. Maybe he could start him talking with minor matters.

"How did ye know there was someone in the old buildin'?" he asked. "Ye walked in there ready for a fight. Inside, before we saw or heard a thing, ye told me in code, 'Others are here.' "

"Tracks in the sand," Benson said. "They'd been swept out, but not well enough."

"What do ye think, Muster Benson? Was the girl in with that gang, or was she really scared of them and kidnapped by them?"

Silence.

Mac sighed and gave it up permanently. The Scot had a hunch that for once The Avenger didn't know any of the answers. He certainly hadn't revealed anything to Mac. And that, too, was a source of bitterness.

They'd come all the way out to the end of Long Island; they'd been jumped by a gang of laughing monsters and left to die in a burning building. And from all this they had learned nothing!

Again the car radio broke in on Mac's pessimistic thoughts. This time it was Josh talking, and this time there was a message of real importance.

"Mr. Benson, news just came from Dillingham Brown's house. The detective in charge there says that Harry Tate has disappeared."

With eyes like pale, lambent jewels, The Avenger flipped on the transmitter.

"Go on, Josh. How do you mean, disappeared?"

"According to the detective, he lowered himself from a window and sneaked off the grounds. Headquarters is sore about it. Tate was not actually under arrest for the murder and robbery, but he was very much under suspicion. Orders were to keep an eye on him. But he managed to sneak away. That makes it look as if he had some guilty part in it."

Benson didn't comment on this. He said: "Go out there, Josh. See if you can find a clue as to where he went. In particular, see if anything points, not to flight, but to a kidnapping."

Mac heard Josh gasp a little, and the Scot felt like gasping himself. What on earth made the boss think of kidnapping? Who would kidnap the dreamy-eyed chemist, and why? But Mac knew he'd get no answers to questions, so he didn't ask them.

The Avenger turned the dial to the regular police band. And in so doing he just missed the voice of a third member of the band, not addressed to him, but to the giant, Smitty.

This was the voice of diminutive Nellie Gray.

Smitty, in an inspired moment, had designed little belt radios for the crime-fighting band. Hardly larger than cigar cases, they were curved to fit the waist and could be worn under a belt so snugly that they hardly caused a perceptible bulge.

Nellie was using her belt radio now, calling Smitty on it. The reason she was calling the giant was that she had uncovered something which she thought she might need help on, but which might not be important enough to transmit to Dick Benson.

Her job had been to try to trace the Browns' maid from the Great Neck railroad station. She'd started there with the same disappointing lack of results which the police had gotten. The agent didn't remember what the girl looked like; he hadn't really seen her face because her mannish hat was pulled so low. She'd gotten on the 12:21 train to town.

Nellie learned that the same train crew would be on the 6:40 train. She waited and took that, then talked to the conductor.

Yes, he remembered the girl who'd gotten on at Great Neck last night. He remembered her because she was the only one at that station. Also, he remembered her because she'd had a ticket for the end of the line, and had gotten off only three stops down from Great Neck.

"You're sure?" asked Nellie, hiding her excitement at this.

"I'm sure," said the conductor. "Say, are you with the police?"

"In a way," said Nellie. Which was true enough. All the members of the band had police credentials entitling them to police support.

"Good. You tell them, then. I was questioned this morning and forgot about her getting off three stations down. I just remembered it a while ago."

Nellie got off where the girl had the night before. She had information even the police didn't have. She hoped it would lead to something.

It was going to lead to something, all right. Something that would curl her silky blond hair for her. But she had no premonition of that.

At the small station which was third down the line from Great Neck, she went to the cab stand. Had any of the drivers seen a girl in a mannish hat, pulled low over her face, come out of the station last night after midnight? Had any of them driven her anywhere?

It looked as if she were going to draw a blank. None knew anything about the girl. But then a cab drew up from a job, and a black-haired, cheerful young fellow jumped out. When Nellie put the question to him, he nodded.

"Yeah, I saw a dame like that. Didn't drive her; she didn't take a cab. She started hoofing it up that street, Maple Street. There's a beer joint up three blocks. See the sign? It's the only thing open around here after midnight. She may have gone there."

Nellie went to the beer joint, drawing a lot of admiring glances as she entered. The bartender's glance was just as admiring. She smiled sweetly at him.

"I'm trying to locate a girl friend of mine," she said. "I think she came in here last night for a minute. Half-past twelve or one o'clock. Were you on duty then?"

"I'm always on duty," the bartender complained cheerfully. "I own the joint. What's your friend look like?"

Nellie gave the description of the maid—rather tall, quite nice-looking, dark hair in a long bob. "She had on a kind of man's hat," Nellie finished. "She always wore it low over her face. You might not have seen her face because of the hat."

That did it, it seemed. The bartender nodded thoughtfully.

"Seems to me I do remember seeing your friend. I remember because of the hat. This girl comes in here alone, see. She's a looker, far as I can tell. But I don't tell very far because I can't see her face. And because I can't, I try to. She gets a nickel from me, and I try to look up under the hat brim, and she turns quick. Say, she ain't hiding from the cops or anything, is she?"

"The cops didn't even know she was alive—last night," Nellie evaded. "You say she got a nickel. For the telephone?"

"Yeah," said the barkeeper. "She went to the phone booth over there, stayed about five minutes, and then went out. I think she headed north, but I couldn't be sure of that."

Nellie headed north.

The trail was spreading out pretty thin now. She was in one of the innumerable suburbs out along the Long Island Railroad. There were probably five thousand homes and other buildings in this one. It seemed impossible to find out which the Brown's maid had gone to, with the little information Nellie had to work on.

The smart little blond reasoned it out at the next intersection above the tavern. One street went left, to the crowded shopping section of the suburb; the other, right, to an apartment section. Straight ahead led a street along which were small homes that grew shabbier and poorer as your eye traveled down the vista.

The shopping section was out. It would be fairly well-lighted even at one o'clock in the morning, and this girl was anxious to keep from being seen and recognized. She wanted only to hide for a few hours and then return to the Brown home as if she'd just come from an evening in the metropolis.

That left the apartment district and the street of single houses as possibilities. Nellie decided to tackle the street first. She went down it two blocks, and suddenly felt a tingle up and down her shapely little back.

When death is your constant companion, and fighting murderers your business, you develop a sixth sense that warns you when there is no tangible reason for it. Nellie felt the slight uneasiness now. *Trouble around here. Watch yourself.*

She had learned long ago, however, that some physical sign was nearly always the reason for these hunches. Some small thing not quite right; some trifle so little amiss that the seeing eye didn't spot it, but subconsciously it was noted. She looked around, trying to spot what it might be in this case.

She was in the middle of a block. On one side, the homes were almost wall to wall. The dining room of each now showed a light, as the evening meal was begun.

On the other side, the lots were bigger. There weren't more than a dozen houses on that side of the block. And at the end was a huge, ugly Victorian house, painted a dull brown many years ago, but now almost totally without paint. It explained the scarcity of houses. It was one of those cases in which the owner of a big house and several acres of land had held out long after the rest of the property around was subdivided, and then had sold in large parcels for more money. And, as is so often the case, the big house itself was deserted, waiting to be torn down.

Nellie's firm little jaw clicked shut. The trifle that she had seen had impressed itself on her enough to ring the faint bell of instinctive warning. Out of the end chimney of this house, a few specks were rising. Not smoke, just a few specks of ash.

The place was boarded up and some of the upstairs windows were broken out. There was a "For Sale" sign in front; obviously the house hadn't been tenanted for a long time.

But someone had had a fire in one of the fireplaces not too long ago, and specks of ash still floated up with the draft now and then.

Nellie clicked on her tiny belt radio. This didn't seem important enough to bother The Avenger with because she had no tangible link between traces of occupancy in a deserted house and the flight of the maid. But just the same, it seemed to her to warrant help in a thorough search.

"Smitty," she said into the tiny transmitter. "Nellie calling. Smitty, this is Nellie. Smitty—"

"Hello, half-pint," came the giant's voice as she held the dime-size receiver to her ear. "In trouble again? O.K. I'll come and haul you out of it. Where are you?"

"I'm not in trouble!" Nellie snapped indignantly.

It was a standard joke of the giant's that he always had to trail her around and save her pretty hide when she got into jams. Actually, Nellie had saved his oversized hide plenty of times, too, but the big fellow conveniently forgot that.

"I'm not in trouble at all. But I think I've uncovered a possibility on the trail of Brown's maid, and I think maybe you'd better come out and lend a hand." She told him where she was. "It's a big old house with turrets and things on it. Only house like it for blocks around. You can't miss it. But maybe you're busy, now?"

"Nope," said Smitty. "Cole and I just ran out of work. We'll be up in a shake."

Nellie put the tiny disks back into her skirt pocket, and settled down, across the street from the big house and down a few doors, to wait till Smitty and Cole came. But waiting was a thing Nellie did very badly.

She bit her smooth red lip in annoyance after ten minutes, looked around and saw that no one was in sight. She hesitated, then decisively started across the street toward the mysterious big house.

CHAPTER VII

Accidents to Order

Nellie lived for excitement. The little blond positively fed on trouble. More than once her impulsiveness had led her into a horrible mess; but, as Smitty said, she'd probably never learn. She'd always be poking her pretty head into places where it was likely to be knocked off.

But she certainly couldn't see signs of real trouble outside the house. She felt pretty virtuous about radioing Smitty at all, instead of just going ahead with an investigation.

The front door of the place had no knob and was nailed tight. She left that and went to the back. There was a knob here. And something else.

On the keyhole plate was a tiny, fresh scratch. A key had recently been inserted.

"So what?" she told herself. "Probably the real estate agent showing a prospect the house."

She took from her bag a tool which each of Benson's aides carried—a flexible length of steel with a tiny hook at the end. Like a flexible crochet needle. With this, she picked the old-fashioned lock.

She opened the door an inch and listened for a long time. Not one sound came from anywhere in the house. She entered noiselessly and closed the door behind her. She left it open a half inch for a possible fast exit and winced as the spring catch squeaked thinly.

She was in the ruins of a kitchen. A mouse streaked across the floor, and she had a bad moment. Nellie could contact gunmen without a blink, but a *mouse*—

The nasty thing went into a hole and left her alone. She drew a ragged breath and went through the next room, a dining room, into a wide, cluttered hall. And there she had her first sign of something wrong.

There was a fresh scrap of paper on the floor among a lot of older tatters. She picked it up. It was the waxed paper that comes around sandwiches put up by a store. It was in the doorway of a big room that must have been a parlor at one time. She went into this room.

A fireplace with a cracked marble facing was at the end, and she placed it as the one from which that chimney led. She hurried to it.

Yes, there had been a fire in it fairly recently. A fire of paper alone, as far as she could tell. There were no wood ashes around. There were ashes of paper there, though, and she whistled soundlessly as she looked at them.

You can make out a little of the original paper after it is burned to ash. And Nellie could make out that financial paper had been fed to the flames.

Stocks and bonds.

The ashes were cold, so some time had elapsed since they were fired; but still, with the breeze stirring outside, some of the fine specks floated up the chimney, so they hadn't been there too long.

"Say from five to twelve hours ago," she breathed. "But I don't get it. Did the *maid* kill the valet, take the stuff from the safe, and come here to hide it?"

Nellie wanted a box in which to put those ashes, very gently, so that they could be studied in the Bleeker Street laboratory. She went toward the stairs. In the attic there might be old boxes. A shoe box for instance.

She went up the stairs, moving silently through habit, not through caution. The danger sense had died down, and now she was annoyed at herself for radioing Smitty. There was nothing here she couldn't take care of all by herself.

She had almost reached the second floor, and in the darkness something brushed softly against her cheek. She checked a cry, and hopped back down a step, hugging the wall. It felt as if a hand had just touched her cheek; as if fingers had lightly stroked it.

But that was crazy. Any reaching hands in this place would go for her throat, not her cheek.

She stood there in the blackness of the stairway for a full minute, then reached slowly upward. Her fingers touched other fingers. It had been a hand!

She wanted to scream, because some things are far worse than direct danger. But she didn't scream. She forced her fingers past the hand—which was ice-cold—and felt to a wrist.

It was a woman's wrist. A girl's wrist. And there was no pulse there. She was dead!

With her breath catching in her throat, Nellie forced herself up to the top step and around the rail. She snapped on the small flash which, with the belt radio, was part of the equipment of each member of Justice, Inc.

The white ray fell on an equally white, cold face. A rather pretty face, even in death, in spite of the terrible discoloration of the throat beneath. It fell on cloudy dark hair in a long bob; on a mannish hat of brown felt lying crumpled to one side of the face.

It was Brown's maid. She would never return, nor would she ever tell police what she might know. She lay there on the dirty floor, with her arm happening to have fallen between bannister uprights so that the stark hand hung over the stairs.

Nellie looked around to see if her purse were near, then snapped off her flashlight with a quick little hiss of breath and retreated down the dark hall.

There had been a sound from the rear. The sound of a door softly opening and closing.

Someone else had stolen in. And it couldn't possibly be Smitty; it would be many more minutes before he could get there.

Nellie debated on attempted retreat out a window over the porch roof, then shook her sleek blond head. She'd stick around. There was no way for the gang to know anyone was inside. And she might overhear something.

"—ought to've waited a little longer before we came back to this joint," a man's sullen voice sounded downstairs as the kitchen door swung open. Nellie heard footsteps in the dining room.

"We had to come the minute it got dark," snapped some other man. "Had to clean the joint out the minute we could."

The steps were in the hall, and Nellie started edging toward the corridor window, immediately behind her. Having her back to it, she didn't see that it was slowly being raised, and that outside it, on the porch roof, was a black blob of a figure.

Nellie stopped retreating. The men downstairs were going into the parlor. The ashes! They'd thought of those, and were going to take them away, along with the cold, stark thing lying with its dead arm hanging over the stairs.

Nellie decided it was time to leave. She'd slide out the window and wait across the street in shadow till Smitty and Cole Wilson arrived. Then the three of them could come back and capture—

"Mmmmp—" Nellie got out. It was meant to be a scream, but just in time a hand clamped over her mouth from behind! Another arm went around her like iron cable, pinioning her arms to her sides.

She'd started to scream when two things flashed like lightning across her mind. One was realization that a ghost of a step had sounded *behind* her, right after the steps downstairs. The other was realization of a ghastly mistake she'd made.

She'd thought these men had no way of knowing she was in the house. She had forgotten that she had left the door off the latch, open a bit, telling a plain story that someone was in the house.

So the men downstairs had put on an act of not knowing someone was in the house, and one of their number had crawled in the hall window and trapped her very neatly from behind.

Nellie tried to yell again and couldn't. She tried to reach backward and catch an arm or something that would allow her to bring into play her deft knowledge of jujitsu. She couldn't manage that, either. But she could, and did, manage to bite the gagging hand over her mouth.

There was a furious oath, and then her captor demonstrated that he was no gentleman. He socked her on the head with a blackjack or something, and she was out of the world.

Nellie slowly struggled back to a consciousness that was very uncomfortable. And it was very dark. She opened her lovely blue eyes.

She was lying, all cramped up, along a wall, on the hard floor. She was in the parlor, with just a trace of light from a street lamp straying in and keeping the room from being in impenetrable blackness. She was bound very tightly, and she was gagged. She was not alone.

Four men sat, near her, on their haunches staring at her in a way that made her wonder if her dress was pulled down far enough. Though the cold menace in their eyes made her realize an instant later that this was a minor worry.

"I don't get it," said one of the men. "You're not a cop. How do you get into this?"

He was obviously the leader, Nailen, the burly fellow with a nose that had been badly broken, at some time in the past, and badly reset so that it was twisted.

"She's one of The Avenger's gang, I tell you," said another of the men—a fellow with babyish pink lips and a chubby pink face. There was fear in his eyes as he spoke the name so hated by the underworld.

"Benson wouldn't be in on this," said the man with the broken nose. "He don't go for straight jobs. He leaves them to the cops."

"Just the same," whined Baby-face, "the dame's in with Benson. I *know!*"

The other two of the four said nothing. They only looked acidly at Nellie. One was tall, gangling, and kept moving his trigger finger all the time. The other was a wisp of a man with premature gray hair and a thin, consumptive chest.

"O.K.," shrugged Nailen. "Hot or cold, with Benson or not, she's got to be fixed."

Smitty, Nellie thought, don't let any grass grow under your feet.

"We could never get *two* stiffs outta here without somebody seein'," protested Baby-face. "It's tough enough to try and cart the one you promoted at Brown's house, without—"

"We won't take two away," said the leader. "This one'll stay here. It's nobody's fault if she dies in an accident, is it?"

"Accident?" repeated the chubby man.

"Sure! Somebody hits her with a car. Runs square over her, all four wheels. Gets away without anyone seeing. It's tough, see? But it's an accident."

"Nailen, you're nuts! Take this dizzy fluff out on the street, bound and gagged, and throw her down and back a car up and run over her? How many people d'you think would see?"

"You dope," snarled the leader. "All we want is for her to be *found* on the street. She don't have to be *run over* on the street."

"Oh," said the chubby one.

"There's a big garage, or an old carriage house or something out back. We toss her on the floor of that, and run the crate we came in over the proper place. Then we wait till no one's around, toss her into the street with the ropes off, and drive off with the other one tucked down in the back of the car."

"Not bad," said the little man with the gray hair. Nellie had begun to wonder if he and the tall, skinny one had voices. "No follow-up on this blond. And nobody ever again sees your girl friend from Brown's. So she finally takes the rap for opening Brown's safe and conking Brown's man. Not bad."

"Oh, Smitty!" Nellie silently urged.

Then something happened that seemed to turn the blood in her veins to ice water. The leader got up; and, as he did so, the luminous dial of his wrist watch showed. Nellie saw the time.

Not fifteen minutes had elapsed since her radio to the big fellow! She couldn't have been unconscious for more than a minute or two, and she'd thought it had been at least a quarter of an hour. Smitty and Cole couldn't possibly get there for another half-hour, Nellie realized.

She had to stall. She made as much noise as she could against the gag, and pointed to her mouth, indicating that she wanted to say something.

The tall, skinny fellow looked at the one called Nailen. The man with the twisted nose shook his head.

"If you take it off, she'll yell."

"Maybe she's got something to say that we oughta hear," suggested Baby-face.

"What?" shrugged Nailen. "We don't care what she's got to say. All we care about is that she'll never say anything. Come on. Bring her back."

So that was out, Nellie thought. No soap on that stall. But she had to pass some more time!

Baby-face got her by her dainty ankles, and the tall, thin man took her by the shoulders. They carried her to the kitchen, and Nailen softly opened the door to the back yard.

Nellie kicked out with all her strength.

The chubby man fell to his knees, rasping out a savage but muted oath. Then he hit Nellie in the jaw, and tightened his hold on her ankles.

Nellie's head rolled groggily. She was in no shape to try any more kicks as they took her to the carriage house.

There was a high board fence around the back yard, rickety but with no planks off. The next houses were fifty yards away, with lots of trees in between. No one could see back there.

Nailen shoved and strained till he got the rusted sliding door of the garage open. Baby-face and the thin fellow dumped Nellie on the greasy, splintery floor, just inside the garage and in the center of the doorway. Nailen went out and, an instant later, Nellie heard the sound of a starter and then a car motor.

A moment afterward she saw a big bulk roll smoothly toward the open doorway. She was lying straight across the doorway. The car slid toward her, with its front tires, to her wide eyes, looking nine feet in diameter. They almost touched her!

With a convulsive movement, Nellie snapped around lengthways, so that the car straddled her. Baby-face swore, and Nailen leaned out the car window and looked back. He saw what had happened and swore, too.

"You damn fools!" he raged. "Hold her, can't you. She's as slippery as an eel!"

He backed the car for another try. This time Baby-face held her head, and the thin man clasped her legs, ready to release her at the last minute. The fellow with the wispy gray hair was plucking at his lips with shaking fingers and looked sick.

The car rolled forward a second time.

So this is it, Nellie thought. All of us have played around with the grave. This time it catches up! This—

The rolling car stopped. "What the—" came Nailen's bewildered voice at the wheel.

"There's a beam under your rear wheels," Baby-face called softly. Then he stopped, realizing there'd been no beam there before.

The realization came too late to do anybody any good. Something like lightning on two legs streaked up to the open car window. A long arm snaked in and coiled around Nailen's throat.

The car jerked as his foot slid off the accelerator. It climbed halfway up the twelve-inch beam under the rear wheels, looking as if it would climb all the way and rush forward on Nellie. Then it stalled and rolled back.

Meanwhile, Baby-face and the two other men jumped to help Nailen. At that moment, a figure so gigantic that it must have looked to them like King Kong's, charged in. It scattered them in all directions.

"Strangle that guy, Cole," Smitty yelled.

Wilson promptly drew Nailen clear through the car window and threw him to the ground. Smitty, having saved Nellie by sliding the big beam under the wheels just in time, now tore at her bonds to free her.

That was a strategic mistake. The giant should have finished his mopping-up maneuvers. But the sight of Nellie lying there bound was more than he could take. He was crazy about this blond half pint, though wild horses couldn't have dragged an open admission from him. So his first instinct was to help her.

And in that instant, the three he'd scattered got into the car on the opposite side and slammed the door.

Too late, Smitty jumped for the car to open it. They'd thrown the lock by then. He started to race around the car.

Baby-face leaned out the other side. He brought the butt of his gun down hard on Wilson's head.

Wilson slumped. Nailen staggered to his feet, shook up but still quite lively. He got into the car and slammed the door just as Smitty got around to *that* side. He started the motor, while Smitty banged at the window, and gunned it back over the beam.

It turned sharply, smashed through a section of the high board fence, and through the next yard to the street. The unholy four had gotten away.

CHAPTER VIII

Guilty Flight

"You big idiot!" raged Nellie, when the gag was off. "You overgrown numbskull! You—"

"Aw, Nellie," said Smitty sheepishly. "When I saw you there all tied up—"

"Why didn't you leave me tied up? Why didn't you nail those four before you started monkeying with my bonds? That's the gang that robbed Brown and killed his servant. They murdered the maid, too; you'll find her up on the second floor in the house. Oh, what I could do to you!"

She stopped. While she was talking she'd been looking anxiously at Smitty's vast moon face to see if he'd been hurt. Where the giant was concerned, her bark was always much worse than her bite.

A point occurred to her.

"How on earth did you get out here on Long Island so soon?"

Smitty looked sheepish again. "To tell the truth, we

were already on our way when you contacted us. We were all done with our job, checking for Brown's bonds and stocks. So I said to Cole: 'Look, Nellie's always getting into a jam. Maybe she's getting in one now. Let's start out toward Long Island, where she's checking railroad stations, and—' "

"Why, you . . . you—" Nellie spluttered. "Always getting in jams! So you start after me! You might at least have waited till I yelled for help!"

"If we had this time?" said Cole, rubbing his battered head. He looked at the garage floor where Nellie had lain while a two-ton sedan rolled toward her.

"Well," said Nellie weakly. She changed the subject.

"We know at least a little something now," she said. "I can identify the gang that broke into Brown's place. I know a little of what they did. The leader, called Nailen—"

"Beak Nailen, eh?" said Wilson. "That helps."

"Nailen played up to the pretty maid at Brown's," Nellie went on. "He got her to open the house to him after she'd somehow learned the combination of the wall safe. After she had opened it, she went to the station and got a ticket for Manhattan. But she got off here, proving that she was an amateur, because she thus gave the conductor a chance to remember her.

"She'd intended to go back to Brown's later, but she got scared. She phoned from a tavern down the line, probably to Nailen's hang-out, and left word to meet her here at this vacant house. Nailen met her, all right; and he was so angry at her for not following orders, and so scared she'd lose her head and give them away, that he murdered her. That must have been during the day, in broad light, or he'd have driven her body away to hide it at once. As it was, he had to leave it, and come back tonight after dark. In the meantime, he burned the financial papers from Brown's safe. Then I got in the way and received the full attentions of the gentlemen."

"Did they laugh?" Smitty said suddenly.

"Huh?" said Nellie, staring.

"They tried to murder you. Did they laugh while they were doing it? You know—had they had any of that dope?"

"I'll be darned!" said Nellie. "I didn't think of that. No, they didn't, Smitty. There wasn't a laugh in the crowd. No laughing-murder stuff here!"

"Guess we'd better report all this to the chief," said Wilson. He tuned in to Bleeker Street. Rosabel's soft voice answered.

"Mr. Benson and Mac are at Mr. Brown's house again, with Josh," Rosabel told them.

Smitty headed the car that way.

As The Avenger and Mac approached Brown's house for a second time that day, all the lights showed in the black of night. The whole place blazed, from cellar to attic, giving an indication of the tension and confusion within.

A detective yanked open the door and, with a gun in his hand, confronted the two when they rang the doorbell.

"Oh, it's you, Mr. Benson," he said when he saw the masklike face with the pale and terrible eyes. He put the gun up. "There's been some trouble out here since you left."

It was the same man who had been left in charge earlier. His eyes were angry, baffled and apprehensive.

"This guy, Tate, did a disappearing act. Right out from under my nose! They'll give me a ride at headquarters for that."

"Were you keeping a close watch on him?" asked Benson.

The man stared sharply at him to determine if he were

being bawled out. Then he saw that The Avenger was merely asking a question.

"Well, pretty sharp," he said. "Tate wasn't under arrest, you know. At the same time, there was enough chance that he was mixed up in this to keep the commissioner interested. He wasn't to leave here, and any phone calls he made were to be traced."

He bit his lip exasperatedly.

"I watched the doors and thought that was enough. When Tate went up to the attic, I thought no more about it. Had a hunch he wasn't in on any part of this, so I didn't even have a small notion he'd pull a sneak out a window. Just goes to show—always believe a guy's guilty till he's proved innocent."

Benson didn't bother to point out that this was directly opposite to American legal practice. He asked: "There was no sign that Tate wanted to get away?"

"None," said the man. "He went up to the attic. Your man, Newton, came and said he wanted to see him. I sent him up to the attic. Tate wasn't there. That's all there is to it. Boy, will I get taken for a ride over this!"

Josh, it appeared, was still up in the attic. Dick and Mac went up there.

Harry Tate had converted Brown's attic into a fairly efficient little laboratory. You could picture him up there under the eaves, striving to perfect an anaesthetic pill that could be administered orally and swiftly in a battlefield operating tent. And never quite getting the result he wanted. Coming up, instead, with the bizarre laughing-murder drug described at Bleeker Street.

Josh greeted The Avenger and had, as might be expected, more to offer than the detective.

"Mr. Tate must have gotten away just before I got here," he said. "He went out this window." He pointed to a dormer window against which a great branch of a tree almost leaned. It would be easy to get down that tree from the top floor of the house. "There are bits of bark scraped off."

"How do you know he got away just before you came?" Mac asked.

"The plainclothesman downstairs had talked to Tate less than an hour before I got here," Josh said. "But there is another hint as to the time. Tate made up a batch of some kind of stuff a very short time ago. This beaker proves it."

Josh handed a thin glass vessel with a pouring lip to The Avenger. There was a whitish film in the bottom, and the film was still just a little moist. The film went two thirds of the way up the side, proving that quite a large batch of the stuff—whatever it was—had been made.

The Avenger took a small vial from a pocket, to scrape a sample of the film into it for future analysis. Josh smiled and gave him a vial already prepared.

"Would that be a batch of this laughing stuff he'd made up and gone away with?" wondered Mac.

"Probably," Benson said. "But what seems to be completely without explanation is—why he made it up at all."

Mac didn't see where this made any difference, but he didn't say so. The Avenger was intensely interested in the fact—the glow of his pale, icy eyes revealed that—and that was enough for the Scotchman.

There was a commotion outside, and Mac looked out the dormer window through which Tate had climbed to escape. It faced the street, and he could see the lights of a car coming up the drive. Then there was the sound of the downstairs door being opened, and the sound of voices.

"That's Brown," said The Avenger.

He went out and downstairs.

In the hall, Brown was talking to the detective and

looking surprised, confused and a little angry.

"I was stopped at my gate," he said. "Three men out there searched my car. There seem to be men all over the grounds looking for something. What's the idea?"

The detective opened his mouth to tell Brown what the men were searching for, but The Avenger cut in smoothly.

"Do you mind? I'd like to have a few words with Mr. Brown."

The detective nodded, and Benson preceded Brown into the fateful library from which the equally fateful contents of that safe had been taken.

"There are men around," he began, "because Tate has left here, secretly, and without police permission. They're trying to pick up his trail."

"Tate left?" said Brown. "The young idiot! That will make him look guilty of this."

"Are you quite sure he had no hand in this robbery?"

"I *know* he didn't!" Brown checked himself. "Of course, I'm sure. He . . . he just wouldn't do a thing like that," he concluded lamely.

The Avenger looked satisfied with the answer. "You have no idea where he would go?"

"None at all," Brown said quickly.

Dick's colorless, glacial eyes looked deep into Brown's, to the latter's obvious discomfort. The pupils of Brown's eyes didn't seem quite normal.

"Well," The Avenger said quietly, "it wasn't about Tate that I really wanted to see you. I wanted to speak about your daughter. I have reason to believe she is in deadly danger."

He told in a few words about the trip out to Long Island. Edna had said she could lead them to the hiding place of the loot. There had been trouble, no loot, and the girl seemed to have been kidnapped.

Brown's face slowly drained of all blood. It got as white

as paper. He moistened his lips, and when he spoke his voice had a dry, croaking sound. But his words were astounding.

"I don't know what silly idea she had in her head when she led you out there, Mr. Benson. And I don't know whom she went away with, but she's safe now."

"You're sure?" said Benson.

"Yes. I . . . I just talked to her. Just before I came home. She is perfectly all right."

The Avenger nodded. "Thank you," he said.

Brown went up to his room, and Benson got Mac and Josh.

"Josh," he said, "I believe Brown may leave here in a few minutes. I want to have him trailed. He may be in a hurry. Don't lose him!"

The Avenger turned to Mac. "I think we've gotten about all we can here."

They got into the car again, and The Avenger went to the home of a friend of his about ten miles away. The man with the awesome, pale eyes had thousands of friends, in all walks of life, and, seemingly, everywhere on earth. This time it was the head of a real-estate firm he sought out.

The man's name was Warbough. He was about sixty and shrewd-looking. He was overjoyed to see Benson.

"Dick! Come in! What can I do for you?"

"I want to know who owns a certain piece of property out near the end of Long Island," Benson said. He pored over real-estate-subdivision maps which Warbough spread out for him and located the plot on which was the ancient building where he and Mac had nearly been fried.

"That one," he said.

Warbough looked up in a book the number printed on the plot. "It belongs to an amusement corporation," he said. Then he laughed. "That is, if anyone on earth but you asked the question, that would be the answer. And it's true. But the amusement corporation is one man—a very big shot indeed. William Xenan, to be exact."

"Xenan!" exclaimed Mac. "Why, that's Brown's ex-partner."

"Yes," said Warbough. "The famous Mr. Xenan. I guess he bought the property intending to expand it. But now he's worth twenty or thirty million dollars, and it's too small to bother with. I guess he's even forgotten he owns it, by now."

The Avenger didn't say anything, but the look in his ice-pale eyes seemed to indicate a wonder as to whether or not the wealthy Mr. Xenan really had forgotten it.

It was a few minutes later that Josh's guarded words came over The Avenger's belt radio.

"I followed Brown. He left a few minutes after you did, and went to Westchester. Great big home. Makes his own house look like somebody's garage. The name of the man who owns the house is Xenan. I'm going to try to find out what goes on."

The radio went dead.

CHAPTER IX

Blond Ingrate

Brown *had* been in a hurry when he left his house. He'd gone like the wind to the great home from which Josh furtively reported. Josh had had the devil of a time keeping him in sight. Brown's stop in Xenan's gravel driveway was so abrupt that the tires of his car had slid a dozen yards.

Josh left his car half a block down and went toward the Xenan grounds like a black shadow in the black night. He reached the hedge just in time to see Brown hurrying in the doorway, and passing a surprised-looking servant. It was then that he'd radioed Benson.

After that, Josh squeezed through the hedge and went toward the house.

Halfway there, he stopped, and his head went back in a strained, listening way. He thought for a minute that he had heard something that he distinctly did not want to hear. A high, thin laugh from somewhere in the blackness beyond the house.

He listened for a full minute, with sweat cold on the palms of his hands. But he didn't hear it again. He decided that he hadn't heard it in the first place. It had been so faint, it must have been his imagination.

He went on to the house.

Xenan's house was a mansion. It must have had forty rooms in it, Josh decided. He wanted to overhear what Brown and Xenan were talking about; but he didn't see how he was going to know which of the many chambers they were in without getting into the house himself.

That looked harder than getting into the Bank of England.

Then Josh saw light blaze in a series of windows on the first floor and to the left. He went there and looked in a window that had countless small panes, leaded, like the windows of a church.

He was looking into a sort of lounging room. Probably it was considered small in this place of vast drawing rooms and reception halls; but it was big enough to effectively dwarf the two men in it.

These two men were Brown and a fellow a bit younger, with iron-gray streaks in dark, bushy hair, and with a hawk nose and ruthless jaw that proclaimed him as the mansion's owner, William Xenan. You could look at that powerfully chiseled face and see how the man had risen in six short years from being Dillingham Brown's well-to-do partner to being one of the richest men in America.

Through a small pane, Josh saw Brown shake his fist at Xenan, and then, suddenly, draw a gun! He held the gun poked into Xenan's stomach. The look on his face showed that he was not fooling. The look on Xenan's face showed that he knew it.

Josh reached into a pocket and whipped out a listening device which The Avenger had invented. It was simple in appearance, a kind of vacuum cup with a wire trailing from it. The principle of the stethoscope had been used, plus the amplifying power of the tiny tubes in Smitty's belt radios.

Josh coupled the wire to his radio receiver, affixed the suction cup to the window, and listened. The voices of the two in the room leaped into audibility.

"Keep your voice down, you fool!" Xenan said to Brown. "There are a dozen servants in the house, and every one of them listens at keyholes.

"I will not keep my voice down!" Brown said harshly. But he did lower it, perhaps without realizing. "I want to know—"

"*I* want to know why you burst into my house and shove a gun in my stomach!" snapped Xenan.

"You haven't the faintest idea, of course," Brown said sarcastically. "You devil! For fifteen years you've—" He stopped, and made a palpable effort for self-control.

Josh practically crawled inside the listening cup, he was so eager to hear. He had a hunch he was on the edge of discoveries that would solve this whole case. But he was not to hear any more.

The next sound he heard was not from inside the house. It was from outside. It came from a little behind him, and this time it was unmistakable. No imagination this time.

It was a high, wheezing laugh, as if someone had just heard the funniest joke ever told. It was joined by the laughter of others. How many others, there was no way of telling.

Josh whirled, with the listening device hanging from the window. He saw dark forms leaping toward him in the night. And as they came these men laughed; laughed till shivers ran down his spine.

Josh breathed sharply and did some leaping himself. Toward the hedge. But more dark forms darted up in front of him. He tried to swerve back again, toward the house. A laughing maniac tripped him. Two more men lit on top of him, chuckling with laughter, wheezing with laughter.

Josh could fight like a panther when he had to. He did so now, flailing out with powerful fists, knocking the two off him.

He got to one knee, heard glass crashing. He looked toward the house. The window at which he had listened had been smashed in. He saw three laughing figures climb into the lighted room and start for the two men within.

Then he didn't see any more.

One of the men he had hit came boring in again. The man had a dislocated jaw, but seemed not even to know it. He struck at Josh with a clubbed gun. It nicked Josh's head.

He swung again and this time connected more squarely. A couple of million Japanese lanterns caught fire in Josh's head and then burst, leaving behind it the blackness of unconsciousness.

Josh had been taken for quite a long ride. He knew that, in a hazy kind of way. He had been dumped somewhere at the end of it, and then somebody had kicked him in the head. At least it had felt like that; and if he ever caught the guy, he was going to make him sorry.

He'd slid into unconsciousness again, after that. Now, he was coming out of it.

The first thing he listened for was the terrible, maniacal laughing. He didn't hear any. In fact, he didn't hear anything at all, for a moment.

Then he heard soft breathing, right next to him.

He opened his eyes with a jerk. There was a person next to him, all right. But not a dangerous one. It was a girl, quite pale but quite good-looking, who regarded him with big scared eyes over a broad strip of adhesive tape which kept her from crying out. She had ash-blond hair and wide, amber-colored eyes.

Josh tried to say something and realized there was adhesive tape over his mouth, too. He could feel the sting and draw of the stuff now that his mind was called to it.

He took stock of the situation in which he found himself, and discovered that he was sitting on a cement floor. Probably it was a basement floor, because he saw no windows and the only light in the place came from a hanging electric bulb.

He was handcuffed, he found, and the links between the cuffs were passed around a steam or water pipe next to a wall so that he couldn't have moved away without taking the pipe with him. His legs were not bound. Why should they have been? He wasn't going anywhere.

This was the way the laughing murderers had left him. Josh wondered who the girl was. He hadn't met Edna Brown, yet, so he didn't know that this was she.

She couldn't get her gag off because her hands were bound behind her with telephone wire. But Josh could hold his face close to the pipe and rip his off with ease. It was a bad sign. It told that the men who had imprisoned him and the girl here didn't care if they got rid of the gags or not; didn't care if they yelled their heads off. That meant they must be a long way from help.

Overhead, Josh could hear someone moving around. He listened apprehensively for the terrible laughter, but there still was none. Instead, he heard somebody moaning, and then heard somebody else growl, "Oh, shut it off, will you?"

The words were muted through the floor, but the fact that they could be heard at all indicated a cheap construction.

Looking around, Josh saw that the cement floor and walls were quite new-looking, as was the electric cord on which the light was dangling. He guessed they were in the basement of a brand-new subdivision house somewhere, the kind they put up by the hundred and sell on easy terms.

Josh leaned his cheek hard against the pipe, got an end of the adhesive gag in his cuffed hands, and ripped it off with a backward yank of his head. He breathed deeply with relief, and turned to look at the girl again.

"Want your gag off?" he said in a low tone.

She nodded vigorously. She was sitting, her back to the wall, about a yard away. She inched toward him, got her face within reach, then winced as the adhesive came off.

"Who are you?"

Josh told her his name. "With Richard Benson," he added, realizing a moment later that this probably wouldn't mean anything to the girl.

However, it apparently did. It apparently meant a lot. She said, "Oh!" as if he'd hit her.

After a moment, in which she regarded him in a curious sort of way, Josh said, "If you could get your wrists within reach, I might be able to untie you."

She tried it. She strained till her face was flushed, and till she was out of breath. Then she relaxed. There was no way for her to reach her bonds. She sat back and closed her eyes.

"Why have they got you here?" Josh asked.

She kept her eyes closed. At first, he didn't think she was going to answer.

"I don't know," she said finally.

"Who are these laughing hyenas?"

"I don't know that either," she said. But from something in her tone, Josh gathered that she *did* know. Or that at least she could do some close guessing.

He gave up questioning her and looked at the pipe.

If he could unscrew that, he could slip the loop of the handcuffs over it and be free—

There wasn't a chance of unscrewing the pipe. But there was no reason why he shouldn't *pretend* to unscrew it. They might hear upstairs and rush down to investigate.

Josh stood upright, with a bit of effort. The ceiling was so low that his head almost touched it. The girl watched him with fearful, perplexed eyes. He turned his hands a little, letting the handcuff links scrape around the pipe. It sounded very much as if it were being unscrewed; and the grating noise should carry all over the house on radiators and pipes.

Josh had made the methodical, regular grating noise only three or four times when there was a yell upstairs. "Hey, what goes on in the basement?"

"What do you mean, goes on? What could go on, the way those two are taken care of?"

"Sounds like that string bean down there was working on the pipe. Unscrewing it!"

"Nobody could unscrew that—"

"Anyway, you go and have a look. Fast!"

Josh stood perfectly still as the basement door was wrenched open and somebody tumbled down the stairs. A flat-faced fellow with a toothpick between his lips stopped at the foot of the stairs, looked belligerently at Josh, and then came toward him. Josh looked blankly at the wall and stood with his huge feet close to the pipe, as if hiding the base of it.

"What're you doin' down here?" the flat-faced man challenged.

"Nuthin'," said Josh, slipping into the slow, dimwitted drawl he used when he wanted to get somebody off guard.

"Are you unscrewing that pipe?"

"Ah guess nobody could unscrew that pipe," Josh said, moving his feet closer to the base of it.

"What are you trying to hide, there?" the man said, catching the small movement. "Let's have a look. Maybe you *are* working it loose."

He took a compact blackjack out of his pocket and stepped close to the pipe and Josh.

"Move those feet of yours," he commanded. "I want a look. A good look."

Josh stood still. The man prodded him with the blackjack.

"Come on. Move!"

Pretending great reluctance, Josh moved his feet from the base of the pipe. The man bent down close to get "a good look."

Josh brought his bound hands down the pipe like lightning, and with all his strength. There was a clunk as the left cuff hit solidly on the back of the man's skull. And that was that.

He sagged to the floor, and Josh grunted with triumph and stooped down. He could just get his hands on the man's coat. With the power of his fingers alone, he inched the body along till the pockets came within reach.

"Hey, Harry," someone called upstairs. "Find anything?"

Josh felt frantically in a coat pocket. They'd come down here fast when they found no one answered that call. But if he could get the handcuff key—

There was no key in that pocket. In fact it was two to one this man didn't have the key at all; there were at least two more men upstairs. Josh began edging the limp body around to get at the other coat pocket. And something fell from a vest pocket attached to a thin chain. It was the key.

"Harry!" came the yell from upstairs, with more urgency.

Josh got the key between his solid teeth and inserted it in the lock. He turned his head. There was a *click!*

More swift steps sounded on the basement stairs. A man lit on the cement floor after taking the last four steps at a single jump. He stared, bug-eyed at the unconscious figure on the floor, gaped at Josh, then reached frantically for a gun.

Josh catapulted toward him like a black streak. The man had just gotten the gun clear of its holster when a swinging handcuff smashed his right wrist, and he dropped the weapon. A dangling handcuff can be a terrible thing, as more than one law officer has found out.

The man yelled. There were answering shouts upstairs. More men were in this place than Josh had dreamed. Whatever number there was, crowded for the stairs.

Josh swung again with the cuff, and the man went down to join his friend in slumber on the floor.

A gun roared like thunder in the confined space. Josh heard plaster crack in the wall near his head, heard the girl scream. There was another shot, covering the descent of four men into the basement. Then there wasn't any more shooting: Josh was shuttling around among them so fast it would have been like trying to hit a shadow.

That tall, sleepy-looking Negro was everywhere! He got a man on the head with the cuff, ducked, danced right and left while guns sought to line on him, hit another man, darted back. In a space of about eight seconds three men were on the floor and the fourth, with a swollen, dislocated jaw, was running frantically for the stairs.

He didn't reach them. Josh caught him in a flying tackle, and he went down. Josh bumped the man's head once against the floor, and he stayed down.

A large stillness filled the basement. In it, the girl's fast breathing sounded loud. Josh looked with a not un-justifiable pride at all the figures littering the new floor, and then stepped briskly to the man at the pipe. His first victim.

He got the little key and removed the second handcuff. He looked around for a moment.

"Say, didn't this guy drop a blackjack?" he said.

He didn't see it, so he went to the girl.

"I'll untie you now. This crew will have a car some-where near and we can get away in that. I wonder where we are."

He got her hands loose, and bent to untie her ankles. The telephone wire was stiff and it took him a moment.

"I wonder where that blackjack is—" he began.

Then he found out.

There was a padded crack on his long-suffering skull that seemed to force his eyeballs right out of their sockets. He pitched forward, and the girl got up and ran! She'd had the little sap hidden under her skirt, and to express her deep appreciation of Josh's bravery in laying the gang low, and her profound gratitude for being set free by him, she had hit him over the head with all her lithe strength.

Josh moaned and wobbled to his feet in a few seconds. He got to the stairs with a great deal of difficulty, and staggered up them. He teetered through new and vacant rooms toward a door.

There was the sound of a racing motor, then the hum of gears. He opened the door and got out to the street in time to see a car speed off to his left. He gritted his teeth on his opinion of the ash-blond ingrate and looked around.

Nothing but new and untenanted houses, vacant lots

and skyline. He had no notion where he was, but he guessed it would be a long, long walk to transportation of some kind.

It was.

CHAPTER X

Girl Trouble

Smitty thought this was about the weirdest affair, this business of the laughing killers, that they'd worked on yet. They went here; they hurried there. They fought a gang of rats that sometimes laughed like maniacs and sometimes didn't.

There was no logic to it. Weird was a mild word for it. Yet, the giant had an uneasy hunch that it wasn't at all weird to The Avenger. He felt that behind the pale, glacial eyes, in the appalling brain, a pattern was already clearly forming.

They were all up in the big Bleeker Street headquarters room. Josh had just finished reporting, being pretty resentful about it when he came to the ingratitude of the blond, whom Dick Benson had identified for him as Edna Brown.

The Avenger turned to the door. None of the rest had heard any sound, but his quick ears had caught one. The door opened and Mac came in. He wore a lab coat over his bony frame.

"Did you analyze the sample from the beaker in Tate's laboratory?" Dick asked.

Mac nodded. "And found nothin' to get excited about, Muster Benson. Unless there's somethin' there that I haven't the knowledge to locate."

"If you can't locate it, it isn't there," Dick said quietly. The Scot reddened with pleasure. "What did you find?"

Mac shrugged. "Laughing gas. To be more specific, the scrapings from Tate's beaker seem to be nitrous oxide, obtained by mixing solutions of hydroxylamine hydrochloride and sodium nitrite in the usual manner. Then it was cooled under presseure to a liquid, boiled, then evaporated to form a white solid. Which would be yer laughin'-gas pills."

Benson said, "Just nitrous oxide. Laughing gas solidified into pills. That would produce a mild form of intoxication, a semi-immunity to pain, and perhaps increased physical strength for a short time. Cases of that have been known. But it would not account for amplifying the murder lust that lies in all men. There was no trace of any other drug, Mac?"

"If there was, I missed it." The bony Scot shrugged.

The Avenger paced slowly up and down one end of the enormous room, eyes like frozen jewels in his mask-like face.

"I think I begin to get some of this," Nellie said hopefully. "Beak Nailen and his gang robbed Brown just for the money and jewels they knew were in the safe. Then they saw the formula that came with the loot and realized that they had something big. They had something they could feed to gunmen that would make them brave as lions, immune to pain, and would deaden their conscious wills enough so that when they were told to kill someone, they'd go out and do it without question."

She looked at The Avenger, but Dick was still pacing and she didn't know if he was listening or not.

"Nailen trailed Brown the next day and saw that he came here for help. He fed some of the pills to a man of his, and sent him to the drugstore to kill Mac and Wilson before they could start fighting his gang. Then Nailen had Edna Brown lead the chief and Mac to a hideout to kill them, too. A preventive war, you might call it. Only both tries failed. And the attempt on Josh's life failed."

Smitty shook his head, also looking sideways at Benson.

"You don't explain enough," he said to the diminutive blond bombshell. "If Edna was in with the gang, why did they snatch her and stuff her down a cellar, bound hand and foot? And how did Nailen make up a sample from Tate's formula so fast? He got it at midnight and had pills ready the next morning."

"Maybe there were sample pills with the formula in the safe," Nellie said.

Then they both gave up. The Avenger was paying no attention at all. He couldn't be made to talk, which showed that there were still too many unsolved riddles in his mind. Too many for discussion.

He did say a few words at last, but it was with an air of talking to himself rather than to them. And he didn't answer questions; he asked them.

"Brown insisted he knew his daughter was safe because he had 'just talked to her.' But he couldn't have talked to her, since she was held prisoner in a basement at that time. So he lied. Why?

"The moment he could, he hurried out of his house and went to the home of his ex-partner, Xenan. He pulled a gun on Xenan; he was furiously angry. Why?

"At just the wrong moment for us, the laughing killers caught Josh and took him away. How did they know he was at Xenan's? They couldn't have trailed him from Brown's house. If they'd been hanging around Brown's place, the police, in searching for Tate, would have discovered them.

"Tate fled though he knew it would make him look guilty. Why?

"Just before, he made up a large batch of his sinister pills. What for?"

Smitty wished Dick could answer these things. If he could, the case would be broken. But he couldn't.

There was a soft buzz. It came from a table near the center of the room. On the table was a small black box that was far more complicated than it looked. It was another product of Smitty's radio genius—a small television set that showed anyone in the vestibule downstairs. The buzzer showed that someone had rung their bell.

The giant went to the set.

"Did you say Edna Brown was an ash-blond?" he said.

Benson nodded.

"Amber-colored eyes, extremely good-looking?"

Nellie sniffed jealously. Dick nodded again.

"Then it looks as if she's downstairs, now. In which case, maybe we'll get the answers to a few of our questions."

Edna Brown was quite pale, and there were smudges of exhaustion under her pretty eyes. Her hands trembled in her lap, in spite of all her efforts to hold them steady. But she was quite self-composed as she faced the members of Justice, Inc. She looked at Josh as if she'd never seen him before, though she must have remembered the man who had freed her.

"I came to you for help," she said steadily.

"Well! You've got a nerve," Nellie gasped. "After leading Mr. Benson and Mr. McMurdie into a trap that almost cost them their lives!"

"And after hitting my Josh on the head!" Rosabel added vindictively. Where her Josh was concerned, she was a savage.

"I'm not asking for help for myself," Edna said. "I'm asking for my father. He has been taken away somewhere. I'm afraid they'll kill him."

"Who are 'they'?" The Avenger shot at her.

She paused for an appreciable instant. Then: "I don't know," she said.

"What makes you think anyone has taken him anywhere?"

"I can't find him," said the girl. "I've tried everywhere. I learned that he went to Mr. Xenan's place last night. It seems he was talking with Mr. Xenan about some matter, and men broke in. They knocked Mr. Xenan out —he has a big lump on his forehead—and they took Dad away. That's all I know."

"That's not very much," Mac said sourly. Mac was a pretty tough nut for the charms of women to crack. Smitty was not so impervious.

The giant smiled nicely at the ash-blond while Nellie glared daggers at him.

"Apparently the same gang that caught you at Long Island and then caught Josh at Xenan's now have your father."

"Apparently," was all that Edna said.

"I don't understand why you come here for help," Nellie persisted. "You've been pretty rough with Justice, Inc., so far."

"I didn't want help, then," Edna said. "I wanted you all to keep out. I was afraid—" She stopped.

"But now you do want help?"

She nodded. "Now my father's life is in danger. That makes everything different."

The Avenger's eyes were like colorless holes in his calm countenance.

"Will you please tell me exactly what was in your father's wall safe?" he asked.

"My mother's jewels," Edna said steadily, "quite a lot of cash, and, according to Dad, Harry Tate's formula."

The Avenger indicated a box on his desk.

"In there are ashes," he said. "They are the ashes of papers burned by Nailen and his gang, the men who robbed the safe. There are ashes of stocks and bonds, which Nailen must have decided he didn't dare risk disposing of. There are ashes of insurance policies. There are ashes of several letters, which were readable enough to tell us that they were important but quite regular—nothing a crook could use. There are ashes of a formula."

"They . . . burned the formula?" Edna gasped. Then she nodded. "I see. They must have copied it, so the paper itself, Harry's regular letterhead, wouldn't be incriminating."

"Possibly," said Benson. "That was all we found, anyhow."

"If you know who robbed the safe," Edna said hopefully, "then you know who kidnapped my father and knocked Mr. Xenan out. Please—let's go after them at once!"

"Sure," growled Mac. "Go after the skurrlies, but where?"

Benson went to his desk and picked up a phone. "Perhaps Xenan can help us out. He must have seen the men who attacked him and Brown."

The Avenger called Xenan's home. They all heard the phone ring and ring and ring. No answer. That was odd, when you considered that a dozen servants should have been around to answer.

"Must have a wrong number," said Smitty.

The Avenger dialed again, but it was not a repeat on Xenan's house phone. It was his office number.

A sleek secretarial voice stated that Mr. Xenan was not available. In fact, he was out of town. He had left an hour ago for Florida, where he intended to stay for at least a month.

"What part of Florida?" Benson asked.

The secretary didn't know. Xenan wanted a complete vacation—no telegrams, letters, phone calls—so he hadn't said where he was going.

"How did he go? By train?"

"I think it was by plane," the secretary said vaguely. "But I'm not sure."

It was certainly out of the ordinary for an extremely wealthy man, with all sorts of pressing business interests, to go off at a moment's notice to some far place where he couldn't be reached.

"Did Xenan come to the office to tell you this?" The Avenger asked.

"No, sir. He phoned."

"You're sure it was Xenan who phoned? Sure it was his voice?"

The secretary gasped in astonishment. "Why, of course, I'm sure!"

Benson hung up. He faced Edna Brown. "Did you talk to Xenan personally?" he asked.

"No. When I heard that my father, the last anyone had seen of him, had gone to Mr. Xenan's house, I telephoned there. It was quicker than going personally. I talked to Mr. Xenan. I'm sure it was he. He told me about the attack last night and the bump on his head."

"Did he say he was going away in a hurry?"

95

"No," said Edna Brown.

The Avenger got to his feet, lithe as a tiger, moving with incredible rapidity.

"I think we'll pay a visit to Xenan's house," he said evenly. "Miss Brown, you stay here, please. Mac, Smitty, Cole, please come with me."

The four left the headquarters room. Nellie looked at Josh with blue eyes full of disappointment at being left out of the arrangements and anticipation of action soon to come.

"Looks like they're expecting trouble," she said.

Josh nodded. "Yes. Otherwise the chief wouldn't have had all three go with him. Well, it'll take an army to make a dent in those four!"

There, just about, was an army, in the end.

CHAPTER XI

The Fourth Door

Smitty stared at the vast stone pile which was Xenan's house, as they drove up toward it along a quarter-mile gravel lane. The shades were drawn and the place looked alone and bleak.

"Servants dismissed too," the giant mused aloud. "Otherwise somebody would have answered our phone call. Fast work, to pack, let the servants go and beat it to Florida in an hour's time."

The Avenger said nothing. He stopped the car openly in front of the big door, and the four got out. It was queer. Even in broad daylight, the place had a dangerous feel.

"Cole," he said to Wilson, "maybe you'd better go back to the garage and servants' quarters and make sure no one is there."

Wilson nodded, bare-headed as usual, with his straight-featured face alert and eager. He went along the side of the house toward the back, and Benson opened the door.

It was almost that fast and easy. The Avenger knew every type of lock and how to open it. And the lock on this door was massive, but not complicated. About twenty seconds sufficed to feel for the catch with a flexible steel rod and throw the bolt.

The three stepped into a hallway so deserted that their steps seemed to echo from four places at once. The ante-room of the house was as big as a baronial hall, with marble balustrades and great pieces of antique oak furniture all over the place. An army could have hidden. But it seems there wasn't any army; a methodical search revealed that.

"What are we lookin' for, Muster Benson?" ventured Mac.

The pale, basilisk eyes roved around the hall.

"This house was cleared of servants and master very suddenly," The Avenger said. "It is just possible that someone cleared it because, for some reason, he wanted to use it, and did not want any observers around. We'll see if we can find such a reason."

For the first time Mac realized that there didn't even seem to be a caretaker here. And that was odd. People didn't usually leave such elaborate homes completely vacant.

They separated and went through the upstairs floors fast. After about ten minutes the three met in the hall again. They'd found nothing suspicious or out of the ordinary.

"Basement," said Benson. Then: "Cole should be back by now."

They listened but couldn't hear Wilson's footsteps. Smitty went to a rear window and looked out toward the garage. No sign of Cole.

"Wonder if anything's happened to him?" the giant said uneasily. "Maybe I'd better go and see."

The Avenger nodded. He and Mac went down the stairs to the spacious basement. Benson told Mac to stay by the stairs as guard, in case someone tried to come down.

The cellar had several doors, Benson saw as he got to the center of it. He tried them. One led to a laundry room, which was empty. Another opened on a playroom, also empty.

The Avenger's pale eyes were narrowed to steely slits, as they usually were when the uncanny sixth sense of the man whispered of trouble nearby. But there was absolutely no tangible sign of danger.

Two more doors opened off the basement. One was different from the other three. It was a solid slab and was obviously very heavy. The Avenger stepped to this one.

A ponderous staple was in this door, and there was a big padlock to secure it. The padlock hung open, however. Benson opened this door.

The other rooms he'd looked in on were lighted by sun from windows. This one had no windows, and it was pitch-dark—so dark that even the pale, infallible eyes of The Avenger could not make out objects for a few seconds.

Benson, as a precautionary measure, took the padlock out of the hasp and slipped it into his pocket so it couldn't be used to lock him in. Then he went into the room.

It was a wine cellar. The smell told him that before he had gone a foot. A searching hand touched bottles in racks and confirmed it. Then he heard a groan.

Groping ahead with hands outstretched, The Avenger touched a light bulb. He snapped it on. Cold light illuminated the narrow, windowless room with the heavy oak door. It lighted up the racks of bottles—and something else.

Two bodies.

The Avenger's hunch that there was something in this

house needing investigation had been right, as were most of his hunches. Cleared it out to use it criminally? Right! The two men in here proved that.

One was Xenan, and the other was Brown.

Brown, of course, Benson knew from meeting the man. Xenan he knew from pictures seen many times in newspaper pages. Brown was the one who had moaned. He lay on his back, limp, deadly pale, with matted hair where blood had oozed from a heavy blow. From his breathing, Benson guessed that he had a fractured skull.

Xenan was breathing heavily, but not moaning. He had crouched in a corner when the light went on, but when he saw who had snapped the switch he gasped with relief and sprang upright.

"Thank heavens," he said devoutly. "I recognize you, sir. I've seen your face in enough publications. You're Richard Benson, aren't you? I heard steps and heard the door open and was afraid it was *them*."

"Them?" said Benson.

"The ones who attacked us last night," said Xenan, voice high and hysterical. "The ones who broke Brown's head, if his long unconsciousness means anything. The ones who threw me in here with him and barred the door."

The Avenger felt the padlock in his pocket. It had not been locked, but its shank in the staple would bar the door, from the inside, as efficiently as if it had been snapped shut.

"I've been in here I don't know how many hours," Xenan growled. "I've yelled till I was blue in the face. In the meantime, these crooks have telephoned around in my name. I heard them talk enough to know that. But where are they now? Are they gone from here?"

"We didn't see anyone around," said Benson.

"We'd better get out of here just the same and take

Brown with us," said Xenan, "before they slam that door on us again."

"A man of mine is out there," said Benson, bending over Brown. Concussion, all right. It was doubtful if Brown would live, along in years and soft from an office life as he was. "He is posted at the stairs so that no one can come down without his knowing it."

The Avenger was probably the greatest crime-fighting machine that had ever lived. But, after all, he was made out of flesh and blood and was human enough to overlook something once in a while.

He had overlooked something this time.

Four doors opened around the big basement room he had first entered: one to the playroom, one to the laundry room, a third to this wine cellar, and to a fourth room, which he hadn't time to explore. It just happened that this was the most important, as far as Dick was concerned.

Many elaborate homes have underground corridors connecting the house with the servants' quarters. This was one of them. There was a tunnel from house to garage, and it was this tunnel to which the fourth door led.

Mac didn't know about this, either. He stayed at the stairs and watched The Avenger. He saw Benson go into the third doorway, knew from the length of time he stayed inside that something important was in there. He listened for sounds indicating that the pale-eyed man needed help, and didn't hear any. So then he relaxed and watched the stairs again.

And while he watched the stairs, that fourth door opened, very slowly, and murderous eyes looked at his back.

It might have been coincidence or it might have been by deliberate arrangement, but at that instant something happened to take the Scot's attention even further from the basement he was in.

Mac heard a faint laugh from somewhere upstairs.

His teeth set hard. He crouched instinctively, for this laugh spelled peril. It was faint, as if suppressed, but it was drawn out, repeated.

He glared up the stairs, too intent to know that the owner of the murderous eyes in the fourth doorway was creeping soundlessly toward him. He heard that maniacal laugh again.

Mac whirled to shout a warning to The Avenger in the wine cellar. He never made the noise.

The figure from the garage tunnel was on him by then; and before Mac could even get his arms up to defend himself, a gun cracked down on his head. The attacker then sped to the heavy door of the wine cellar, slammed it shut, and dropped a thick iron bolt through the staple loop.

That door would have to be broken down, now, before anyone could get out. And no human being without a battering ram, not even The Avenger, could break the massive oak.

The man began to laugh. He stared down at Mac's bony, unconscious length and wheezed with laughter. Laughing, he picked up the bony body and started with it up the stairs.

Like a crazy echo, laughter sounded from the head of the stairs, too. And another man appeared, carrying another body. This was the body of Cole Wilson.

He dumped Wilson in the hall. And half over Wilson's body, Mac was dropped.

"The big fellow?" said the one who'd carried Mac.

"Ha-ha-ha! He's in the garage. Chained him to the wall."

The second man sputtered this out between chuckles and then, shaking with laughter, went to a closet and came back with a vacuum cleaner. He put the hose on the reverse end of this, put a flat attachment on the end of the hose and stuck this next to the crack under the wine-cellar door.

He turned on the motor and the thing began shooting air under the door into the almost-airtight wine closet. Then he poured a colorless liquid, that began to evaporate in misty white fumes almost at once, into the air stream.

"Hee-hee! When they get a couple whiffs of that gas—"

With murderous eyes intent in his laugh-twisted face, the man emptied the small bottle he had tipped over the air stream. The whitish fumes snaked under the door as if pulled by strings.

The man stared at his watch, twitching with laughter, till ten minutes had passed. Then he opened the door.

There were three bodies inside, now, instead of two. All three were limp and still. The man stepped inside, holding his breath as well as he could between chuckles, then caught Xenan by the shoulders. He dragged him out, leaving the wounded man, Brown, and the still body of The Avenger where they lay.

"Ho-ho!" laughed the man, glaring at Benson. "So you're the guy everybody's scared of. Haw-haw-haw!"

He pulled a gun and leveled it at The Avenger's head. His finger flexed on the trigger. But not quite enough. Not quite. For twenty seconds that seemed like twenty years, he stood there, with Benson only a half-ounce pull from death. Then he put the gun up, put his other arm around Xenan's flaccid body, and went out, trailing laughter behind him like Satan's plumes.

Xenan was the only one they took from the house.

There was a big sedan in the garage, and when they'd all met there, it was revealed that there were six of them. They crowded into the car.

Hanging limply from one of the garage walls was the enormous form of Smitty. The giant had a deep gash on his head and was still unconscious. Laughing as if nothing had ever been funnier than the sight of the huge fellow spread-eagled against the wall with two pairs of skid chains, the six drove out, taking the wealthy, famous William Xenan with them.

Cole Wilson was the first to recover in the mammoth, baronial front hall. He stirred and blinked. "What—"

His hand drew back from what it had touched, and then he recognized the moveless object.

"Hey, Mac!"

Wilson found a first-floor bathroom, staggered back with a towel soaked in cold water and slapped this against Mac's face. The Scot spluttered and came to.

"Cole! Where's— What happened?"

"You tell me," said Wilson, his handsome face grim. "I went back to the garage and took one step inside. Thought I was being pretty cautious. I heard a laugh, turned, and a house fell on me. That's all I know."

" 'Tis about what happened to me," said Mac. Then: "Say! Smitty went back to find you. Didn't you see him?"

"I saw nothing but stars. Where's the chief?"

Mac answered with a blank look. They ran to the garage. Smitty was just stirring, with dawning realization and fury, against the wall. He roared as he saw the two.

"They hit me with a four-by-four. Or maybe a six-by-six. I didn't have a chance. If I get my hands on them—"

He flexed great fingers in throttling motions. He began fighting the chains.

"Wait a minute," said Wilson, more composedly.

Smitty could have broken loose, all right; few bonds could restrain his gigantic strength. But it was quicker to unfasten him. With this done, the three ran back to the main house with dread in the heart of each.

The Avenger!

There'd been no sign of him in the house; no sound

from him anywhere. The members of Justice, Inc. talked as if they had a feeling that Dick Benson was immortal. That he couldn't be killed. But each knew differently. They knew that some day knife or bullet or rope would cut The Avenger's career short.

Was this the time?

They spread through the house, calling, hunting frenziedly. No sign of the man with the coal-black hair. No trace of the man with the deadly, icy eyes.

They found Brown.

"This man is a hospital case," snapped Mac. "We've got to get him to an emergency operating room quick."

"But the chief!" snapped Cole.

Benson wasn't there, that was all. The gang had gone somewhere. And with them—dead or alive—must be The Avenger.

Feeling numb and dead, as if the mainspring had broken in each of them, they went out with Brown, to drive him to the nearest hospital. They pinned their hopes on Brown. When he regained consciousness and told what he knew—

But this hope was dashed. The doctor at the hospital said: "He may die. I don't know. It's a bad skull fracture. In any event, it may be days before he recovers consciousness."

CHAPTER XII

Private Asylum

The members of Justice, Inc. used gas, themselves, very frequently. With their aversion to taking life, they had found that the best way to knock out criminal opponents harmlessly was with gas.

MacMurdie, chemical genius, had concocted a number of weird gases and with each had worked up chemical antidotes, so that the gases could be used by the little band without rendering them unconscious, too. Finally, the brilliant Scot had combined these into a chemical filter that would absorb *any* gas.

Now, each of The Avenger's crew was always with prepared little nose plugs, saturated with this all-purpose chemical. Also, the men constantly had their coat lapels treated with it, and Nellie and Rosabel their handkerchiefs.

When the laughing murderer sent gas under the door of the wine cellar, it promptly anaesthetized Xenan and plunged Brown into deeper unconsciousness. But not The

Avenger. The instant the acrid fumes stung Benson's nostrils, he simply held his coat lapel up to his nose and breathed through that.

When the man came in and got Xenan, at the end of ten minutes, The Avenger could have felled him with ease. But it suited Dick's purpose better to feign unconsciousness till the man had gone. Then, moving like a pale-eyed tiger, The Avenger slid to the fourth basement door, the tunnel door, and ran silently out to the garage.

The door out there was closed, too. He opened it an inch, saw three men straining to hold upright the vast, inert weight of the giant Smitty while they fastened him with heavy skid chains to hooks in the garage wall.

Dick's eyes were as grim as polar ice under a pale moon, and for an instant it looked as if he would drop everything and rescue his man. But that would obviously have tipped his hand, so he went on. Behind the backs of the straining men he padded soundlessly to the rear of a big car lurking there in the garage. He opened the rear compartment and got inside it, leaving it open a bit in order to see.

After quite a while he heard more men enter the garage, coming from the house. They were not laughing so hard, but there were still the maniacal chuckles to be heard. The car sagged with their weight, and Dick tensed his iron muscles for a desperate fight if necessary.

There was Xenan. It was pretty certain that these men were carting him away somewhere. It would have been natural if they'd crammed the millionaire into the car's trunk; and if they tried that, Benson would be discovered. And you can't go into action very readily from so small a space.

However, the gang apparently decided to ride Xenan in the car, for presently the motor leaped to life. Dick felt the sedan back out of the garage. It whirled, started forward. He felt it jounce as it left the driveway and turned down the street.

There was a long ride, during which The Avenger flexed his supple muscles scientifically to keep them at top pitch in spite of his cramped position. And "top pitch" for Dick Benson meant something!

Now and then, a person is born with muscles that seem to be of a special quality, so that ounce for ounce they are many times stronger than ordinary muscle fiber. Benson's iron body was like this. The Avenger was no more than average height and weighed about a hundred and sixty-five pounds; but even the giant Smitty, with all his tremendous strength, could not bring him to his knees.

The car was miles away from Xenan's house, now. There had been many curves and twists, and the car had bumped and jounced over many types of roads, hard-topped, dirt, gravel. These were back roads. And the car had turned north on leaving the house and had kept that general direction.

They'd come far north, then, into rural Connecticut, over back roads.

Finally the car stopped, and The Avenger tensed again. But it was still, it seemed, not the end of the journey. He heard another motor, off to the left. The men had joined other men here.

During the ride The Avenger had heard nothing but the loud singing of the tires so close to his ears. He could faintly hear voices. But no laughter. The bizarre drug of Harry Tate's invention had lost its effectiveness, it seemed. It did not last long.

Benson, for all the marvelous keenness of his jungle-developed hearing, only managed to catch a few words in a mumble of voices.

"—Nailen. Meet us—"

That was all.

There was a slam of car doors off to the left where that idling motor sounded, the noise of a car being backed around and driven down the road. Then the sedan came to life, too, and took up its northward journey.

This time, just before it stopped, The Avenger heard the hollow rumble of boards under the wheels. And darkness, covering the crack through which he could see a little, told that the car had been driven inside a building. They were at their destination.

The men got out. Benson heard Xenan's dazed voice just once, "Say! Where—" Then it was silent; the sound of footsteps died away. There was utter stillness.

For at least ten minutes The Avenger stayed warily in the trunk. He heard crickets, and now and then a bird. No sound of traffic; no human noises. This must be deep country.

Dick's steely hand raised the lid, ready for explosive action, but he found that none was needed. He got out. He was in a space that stabled two other cars besides this one, and also a queer light truck with solid sides and no rear window.

The sliding door of the place wasn't quite shut. Dick looked out the crack and saw a large expanse of weedy lawn, heavily studded with big trees. Also, he saw a man walking slowly but methodically back and forth across the rear of a huge house. In fact, a house too big to be a house; it was a small inn or something.

The Avenger's gaze went beyond the man who was doing sentry duty, beyond the tree-set grounds and to a wall. It was a high wall, sheer, unclimbable, and the sun glistened on broken glass set in its top. The place was as closed in and closely guarded as a jail.

With comprehension glittering in his big, colorless, inhuman eyes, The Avenger stepped to the odd truck. There was a small wood panel, of the removable type, set in the left door. It said, "McCoomb's Private Sanitarium."

Benson went back to the garage door and watched the sentry at the back of the sanitarium building, timing his trips. He saw that at regular intervals another man stepped into sight and out again at the right-hand corner of the house. Another sentry.

The Avenger got the timing of both, picked an instant when both would be faced in the opposite direction for the longest amount of time; then he darted to the nearest tree.

Trees were friends to The Avenger. He had mapped jungles, explored wildernesses, and sought for treasure in places where no white foot had ever trod before. He was at home in the wilds as few natives ever are. Added to this was his great strength, which could whirl his average-size body through incredible acrobatics as a giant truck motor might power a small sedan chassis.

In a few seconds The Avenger was thirty feet up the tree he had chosen, leaning against its bole so that a person would have had to look squarely at him to see him. And people don't normally lift their gazes that high.

From there, Dick could see into the second and third-story windows of the sanitarium. He saw no one.

Into room after room his probing, pale eyes stared; and each was vacant and bare, looking as if it hadn't been occupied for a long time.

In fact, the whole building looked as if it had lain vacant a long time, and then had been picked up quite recently for some specific purpose—a purpose temporary enough so that it wasn't found worthwhile to renovate or repair.

Benson swung silently from the branches of this tree to those of the next. The big trees formed almost a solid second floor to the grounds; and along this aerial second floor The Avenger moved at will, while under him four men did solemn "guard" duty.

He was able to look into every room in the place, save a couple on the ground floor which had shades drawn. And he saw that, barring possible patients on the ground floor, McCoomb's Sanitarium seemed to have just one customer.

In a third-floor room near the corner was one occupant. The room was almost as vacant as the others, but at least the bed was made up instead of being bare-springed and rusting. On this bed was a figure in a strait-jacket.

The Avenger got as close to this window as he could. The nearest branch was ten feet from the building. It was pushing luck and skill a long way to try to leap across that distance to the sill without being seen from below. But Dick jumped anyway.

Clinging rubber soles thudded lightly and exactly on the sill. Steely fingers caught the sash in time to stop the backward reaction. The Avenger opened the window and walked in.

The man on the bed was Harry Tate.

"Benson!" Tate said. He looked as if he'd have liked to shout it, but he spoke almost in a whisper. "Thank heavens you're here."

Harry Tate was in a bad way. His vague, dreamy eyes were filled with fear. The fresh scars on his face could mean only one thing: cigarette ends had been pressed there. He had been tortured.

He saw The Avenger's pale eyes on the burns.

"They wanted more of my laughing-gas derivative," he said. "When I wouldn't make any more up, they tried to force me to."

Benson only nodded, eyes steely slits in his masklike

face. He began to unlace the straitjacket which held Tate so helpless.

"Don't let them get me again," Tate whimpered. "Did you get in here without being seen? Are you sure?"

"I hope I did," was all Benson offered. "You left the house with quite a bit of the nitrous-oxide pills. Weren't there enough for this gang?"

"Apparently not," said Tate, moving his arms. "They wanted more."

"Is this the same crowd that robbed the safe?" Benson knew that it wasn't the same. He knew that there were two gangs somehow mixed up in this—Beak Nailen's and another. Recent events had proved that. But he wanted to see what Tate would say.

Tate had nothing to say at all. He only shrugged and said he didn't know.

When Benson had Tate's ankles almost loose, he said: "You wouldn't be in this mess if you hadn't sneaked away from Brown's house. Why did you do that?"

"Brown asked me to," said Tate. "And what he asks, I do. I owe him everything."

"Brown told you to steal away from the police?"

"Yes. He told me to bring a fresh supply of the anaesthetic pills with me."

"Was it Brown who had you brought here?"

Tate looked distressed. "I hope not! I've always thought he was tops. Now, if he had this cutthroat crew kidnap me and bring me here and treat me like this—" He shook his head. "I can't believe that, Mr. Benson. I think someone else found out I was leaving and hired a crew to pick me up. I was jumped about a half mile from the house and thrown into a car."

"Who else could find out Brown had asked you to leave? I imagine he'd keep it secret."

"I don't know. He might have told his daughter, that

would be all. And surely *she* isn't mixed up in this."

" 'This'?" The Avenger shot out. "What do you mean, 'this'? 'This' what?"

If Tate was acting, he was doing it well. He sighed and shook his head. "I wish you'd tell me. I go along, working on a new anaesthetic, and all of a sudden Brown's safe is robbed and all hell begins to pop. I don't get it—"

He broke off and listened. The Avenger had been straining his ears for a half minute already. He had heard steps outside, far down the corridor, but coming near.

"Can you use your muscles?" he said in a low tone to Tate. "Circulation restored?"

Tate nodded, looking scared but resolute. Benson went to the window. Keeping to one side, he looked out. There seemed to be no one watching. He looked directly out and down—

There was a sound like that of a giant typewriter, and the eaves over his head began to crumble like the edges of a cake in a rain! Directly underneath the window was stationed a man with the latest in machine guns.

Benson whirled toward the door. To the right, down the corridor, someone yelled, "O.K., break it open!"

To the left came an answer, "Let's go."

The Avenger *had* been seen, in that last long jump to the window sill. And silently, efficiently, the gang had prepared a trap for him. Exit out the window was impossible. And the hall was full of men!

A new sound broke out. It was a high-pitched laugh. It was joined in a devil's chorus by others, in a few seconds. Tate moistened his lips.

"They've taken some of the stuff. Makes a rat as brave as a lion. You can't hurt them; they're stronger than they have any right to be. And they'd as soon kill as—"

There was a bang against the door. It trembled from

top to bottom. Someone had a log for a battering ram, out there in the hall.

Bang! Shrieking laughter greeted the appearance of a crack in the panel. The door couldn't last another half minute, at that rate. Tate stared at Benson with the wild terror of a trapped animal.

CHAPTER XIII

"Don't Kill—Yet"

The Avenger put his lips close to Tate's ear.

"We can't both get away from here. But I think you can, if you act fast. While I keep them busy, you jump across the hall to the opposite room and shut and lock the door. Go out the window on that side and run. I don't think there will be men stationed over there; they're all in on this attack."

Before Tate had time to say anything, Dick went to the door.

Bang! The panel was split badly, now. Enough so that Dick could see out a very little. He saw a backward surge of movement as the ram was brought back for another blow. He turned key and knob in the door and stood flattened against the wall beside it.

Bang—

The door burst off one hinge. But it did more. It flew inward so fast that it almost went on out through the wall on the back swing. And a half dozen men braced for a hard impact tumbled forward, with their hard-swung heavy log, like half a dozen tenpins.

Yelling, laughing even then, as if this was the funniest thing ever, they piled in a tangle on the floor. The Avenger leaped over two of them into the hall. Three men were out there, upright, because there'd been no room for them to help with the ram.

They had their guns drawn, and a second after The Avenger catapulted into the hall, two shot at him. One slug hit his body, protected by the bulletproof celluglass. The other slug—

The first man who had shot screamed with sobbing laughter and fell to the floor with almost his whole throat torn out by the shot of his pal. The other two stared, laughed wildly, and swung on Benson again. But the diversion was the finish for them.

The Avenger got one of them with a blow to the jaw that sent him ten feet down the hall—and out of this world. The other, he caught by the neck.

"Run!" he snapped to Tate, who was standing just outside the door, paralyzed with fear.

Benson's fingers found a nerve center in the man's throat and he pressed. The fellow sagged. By now, two from within the room, yelling with laughter, were coming for Tate.

At this, Tate woke up. He jumped for the door across the hall, swung it open, and ducked into the room there. He slammed the door and the lock clicked. Benson heard the window go up, then didn't hear anything more but the insane laughter as the whole devil's crew of them jumped him.

He actually stood them off for a minute. Two went down, in spite of the fact that the stuff they were doped with made them thrice as hard to knock out as normal men.

Dick got another in the side so hard that he felt ribs crack under his knuckles. But then he was through. The blackjacks and clubbed guns, raining for his head, caught up with him. He fell!

It looked for a moment as if this gang would beat him to pieces, to a pulp, laughing like murderous robots as they did so. But one of them got in front of the prone body and held up his hand.

"Ho-ho-ho! We're not to kill him. Not yet. Ha-ha!"

They picked him up. There were six of them left. Six against one. They carried him down the stairs and out to the yard. There, one of them lifted a heavy iron lid, like a manhole cover.

A pit was revealed, about six by eight and buried five feet deep. It was lined with concrete. Its purpose was revealed when filtering daylight showed a big pump. This was the water supply for the sanitarium, which was beyond the reach of any town water.

The laughing killers threw Benson into the pit. They put the lid down again. Then one of their number went to the garage. He drove out the truck, and ran it across the weedy lawn to the covered pit. Then he stopped it, carefully, so that a rear wheel was on the iron cover.

With the entire weight of the truck holding down the cover, the men left, still laughing like fiends. It was as tight as Alcatraz, that little prison they'd devised on the spur of the moment.

In the pit, The Avenger read the story all too easily from the sounds. The vibration of the ground as a car drove overhead, the sound of the motor, the distressed creak of the iron lid as the great weight came to a stop on it—these outlined a graphic picture.

But Dick dismissed this from his mind for a moment. When he was tossed in, he had landed on something soft, yet unyielding. He felt for his small torch, found it worked all right and turned its beam on the thing.

If he was disappointed, the only thing to indicate that emotion was the slightly increased glitter in his glacial, colorless eyes. His face expressed nothing.

The stirring thing in the pit was Tate!

They'd caught him outside the window.

Tate moaned. "I think I've got a broken ankle from the jump," he said. "And I nearly fell on top of two men who were out there. They are too smart for us."

Benson didn't comment on that. He looked at the ankle. Badly sprained, but not broken. Swiftly, methodically, he bound it with strips from his undershirt. Tate stared.

"You'd think I was going to use this," he said at last. "You'd think I was going some place on it."

"You are," Benson said quietly.

"With that lid overhead held down as it is? I don't know what they put on it, but I could fairly feel it give."

"There's a wheel of a car on it," said Benson.

"And you think we can lift *that* off and—"

"We couldn't possibly lift it up," said The Avenger, and his voice and face were never more expressionless, "but we should be able to pull it down—break the lid—with so much weight on it."

The handle on the lid was an upside-down U of iron. The ends were threaded and had nuts on them. And with the lid in place, the U collapsed down against the thing so that the ends stuck down four or five inches. Benson gripped these.

"Hang onto my legs so I don't just lift myself when I pull down."

Shaking his head, patently sure no such crazy thing could work, Tate grabbed Dick's corded legs. The Avenger pulled.

There was an audible creak, the iron lid dipped down a little in the middle, and then both Benson's and Tate's bodies swung upward with the terrific pulling power of The Avenger's arms.

"Hook your feet under the pump. That's bolted down," Benson said.

Tate did so. The Avenger exerted his magnificent strength again. There was a thin shriek of metal, then a crack like a pistol shot. The lid was cast iron. It wasn't meant to bend. It broke.

The two halves fell clanging to the pit floor, and instead of the lid a wheel and tire suddenly showed, pressing down almost to the axle into the hole.

"We're as bad off as we were before," Tate began. Then he saw that they weren't.

The tire, spread as it was by the pressure, didn't block the opening the way the lid had. There was just room for a small and agile man to squeeze up between the edge of the opening and the tire. Benson did so. He held his hand down and hauled Tate up.

Tate blinked with the sudden sunlight, and with a vast admiration.

"I can see why you're so famous," he said. "Anybody on earth would have thought we'd never get out—"

"No time for that," said Benson. "We have to find that gang again. They went to meet someone. A man named Nailen, I think, from something I heard on the way here."

Tate's forehead wrinkled thoughtfully. "Say! Yes! That *is* the name. After the two at the window nailed me, one said, 'Dump him in the pump; do it quick. We're to go after Nailen with the other guys.'"

Dick nodded. He could fill in the few words, now, that he had heard while he'd been in the trunk, when his car stopped beside another.

The full sentences must have been: "We're after Nailen. Meet us at his place."

But there was no clue as to where that place was.

Dick asked Tate if he had heard anything that might shed light on that, and the young chemist shook his head. He had not.

The Avenger helped him into the truck cab, careful of his bad ankle. Then Benson hooked his dime-size transmitter to his belt radio. He knew even without testing it that it would work all right in spite of the way he had been tumbled around. It took almost a direct hit with a bullet to put one of Smitty's little gems out of commission.

He got Bleeker Street after a minute.

"Chief!" came Mac's voice, tiny in the receiver but registering a wild joy unlike the taciturn Scot's normal lack of emotion. "Muster Benson! We thought ye—"

"I'm all right," The Avenger said. "Some of our jovial murderers have gone laughing on their way to tangle with Beak Nailen's crew. We want them, and we want the Nailen gang. Has there been any word yet about Nailen?"

"There has," said Mac. "The police have no word about them. But we just had a report from a Queens newsboy—said he'd seen Nailen go into a big apartment building there."

"Which boy?" said The Avenger.

"Turkey Doolittle," Mac replied.

"See that he gets anything he wants. What address in Queens?"

Mac's tiny voice gave the answer. "Meet me there, all of you," Dick said.

He put the receiver and transmitter away in a vest pocket. Tate was gaping at him in bewilderment. He'd heard the small voice, too, but it didn't mean much to him.

The Avenger raced the truck motor hard and let the

clutch out fast. The rear axle creaked and the truck lifted almost out of the hole that the one rear wheel was in. At the second try, it heaved from the pit opening and started across the lawn.

Tate said, puzzled, "If the gang that got me isn't the one that robbed the safe—what gang is it?"

Benson said nothing. Eyes jewel-bright, he raced the truck south from the weedy, deserted sanitarium.

"I don't get any part of this," Tate complained.

"It isn't as complicated as it looks," The Avenger said. But that was all.

CHAPTER XIV

Death in Fractions

Night was falling when the windowless light truck, once used for transporting straitjacket cases to McCoomb's Sanitarium, came to a stop a block from the Queens address given by Turkey Doolittle. Benson spoke into the transmitter of his belt radio.

"Benson calling. Smitty, Mac—any of you around the Queens address yet?"

It was Mac who answered with the information that they had reached the place just a moment ago and had stopped out of sight a block in the other direction.

The two parties got together.

They were a grim group now: The Avenger, Wilson, Smitty, Mac, and Tate. That is, everyone was grim but Tate. He wasn't really in on this, as the others were.

"I talked to Turkey," said Smitty. "Bright kid. However, he naturally doesn't know what apartment Nailen is hiding in. Just the building."

"Is Nailen alone?"

"No," said Smitty. "There are three men with him, according to Turkey—a very tall, very thin guy, a chubby fellow with a baby face, and a wispy little guy with gray hair."

The Avenger searched the filing cabinet of his marvelous memory.

"That's all there is to the Nailen gang," he said, "unless he has gathered new recruits. Nailen was never a big shot and never had a big mob. When we get these four, we have the works."

It was noticeable that Dick didn't say "if"; he said "when." There were no "ifs" when The Avenger was on the trail.

At the instruction of Benson, Cole and Smitty went one by one to the vestibule of the building, as unobtrusively as possible. The gang from the sanitarium had quite a head start; it was possible that they were already here. If so, it was no use warning them that Justice, Inc., had arrived.

Mac, also at Benson's instruction, stayed with Tate in a dark doorway across the street to warn of enemy approach or, if necessary, to rush in as reinforcements, if the rest stayed longer than they should in Nailen's place.

The building where Nailen was hiding out was huge. It must have had a hundred apartments in it. The names under the bells in the big vestibule stretched all along the wall, set close together. The three men divided them and began looking. It was Smitty who found it.

"Amos Beaker," he said. "Beak Nailen—Beak—Beaker. It's a chance. Anyhow, we can't search every apartment in the place. Might as well try this first."

Benson's head, with its virile close crop of coal-black hair that contrasted so strangely with the pale eyes, nodded agreement. The three went upstairs, instead of in an elevator, to the sixth-floor rear, which was the indicated position of the Beaker apartment, according to its position in the list downstairs.

They listened at the heavy stair door. There were many sounds—the building was about ninety-eight percent full —but there were none that seemed to come from the corridor itself.

They stepped into the hall. Working with the wordless precision that comes of long cooperation, they split and went to various rear doors. It was Cole who raised his hand. Still without a word, the other two came to the door in front of which he had halted.

They stared at the little name card next to the door: "Amos Beaker." Furthermore, it was written in a backward-slanting longhand, as was the name on the plate in the vestibule.

The Avenger got out a listening device, similar to the one Josh had used at Xenan's palatial home, and fastened the vacuum cup to the panel.

He shook his head to the others, pale eyes like chromium chips in his immobile face. No sound, the shake of the head meant. And yet there should be sound—*some* sound—of a person's breathing, if nothing else, unless the apartment was not that of Nailen, or unless something had alarmed the men and they had fled.

Benson worked with the lock. This was a new building and the locks were good. It took over three minutes to open the door.

There was a large living room opening off a small, neat foyer. There were several doors around the living room, each newly varnished and shiny and untouched. The floor of the room and foyer was the same way—brand-new, shiny, with no trace of anyone's having walked on it or of furniture having been placed on it.

The apartment was vacant, looking as if it had never been used.

The tension went out of Cole and Smitty.

"Nuts!" said Smitty. "Wrong name. Amos Beaker is plainly not Beak Nailen. And Amos Beaker has plainly moved out, without taking his name from the vestibule—"

He stopped. And apparently the realization that flooded him was shared in the same instant by Cole. Benson must have known it right along.

"Wait a minute!" the giant said. "Amos Beaker 'moved out'? Amos Beaker was never in here! No one was ever in here! The new floor tells that. So how come—"

The Avenger had his head down at floor level. From there, the colorless, infallible eyes could see traces of dust in a straight line. The traces led straight to a window. Other, slighter traces, lined toward each door in the living room.

Benson leaped back to the door leading to the corridor. His steely hand caught the knob, turned. He jerked.

The door refused to budge!

He jumped to a living-room door; and, following his lead, though they were still more surprised than startled, Smitty and Cole leaped to the other doors.

They, too, refused to budge.

They were locked in the room so that nothing short of battering a door down would get them out.

Smitty snorted contemptuously. With his great strength and nearly three hundred pounds of brawn, doors were flimsy things. He was used to going through ordinary ones like a tank through an unpropped brick wall.

He rammed his vast shoulder with shattering force against one of the living-room doors.

"Ouch!" he said, looking surprised. The door had quivered throughout its length, but hadn't budged. It was heavily barricaded on the other side.

He started for another door, but then a click caught the attention of the three of them. It was a small sound, about the kind made by an alarm clock just before the alarm goes off.

It had come from the window. They stared that way and saw the window slowly and easily sliding up.

"Somebody's out there!" yelled Cole.

But he had spoken impulsively, as he too often acted, and instantly he realized it. No one could be out there; the building wall dropped sheer for six stories to the street.

He started toward the window, stopped. A small piece of bent tin, like a tiny coal chute, was rising as the window did. It hit about a forty-five-degree slant, and something rolled down it to bounce a little on the floor inside. Then it rolled almost to their feet.

The thing looked like one of the little change cylinders that are snapped from department to department in big stores. It looked also a bit like a tin firecracker, because one end had a fuse that was sputtering gaily.

It was a bomb, and it was going to go off in about two seconds; the fuse had been deliberately shortened so that the thing would explode almost the instant it rolled into the room.

"For the love of—" Smitty mumbled. He thought he yelled it, but the words could hardly be heard.

The giant had been close to death before, but never quite this close, and never to such a violent death. When that thing went off—

He didn't even grab for it. These thoughts had raced through his mind before he could have moved a step. And Cole was paralyzed to immobility, too, by the sure and instant knowledge that no move could be made in time.

But Benson moved!

Like light he flung himself toward the deadly cylinder. With horrified eyes, Cole and Smitty saw that the fuse was too close to the thing for even fingers like Benson's to seize.

The Avenger didn't try to seize it with his fingers. The cold brain behind the pale eyes was like the incredible body that powered it. It worked about three times as fast as a normal one.

With a sweeping movement The Avenger caught up the cylinder and pressed it to his face. The sputtering had stopped as the burning fuse reached the metal wall of the homemade bomb. And the instant arrived when the spark should ignite whatever explosive was in it. But at this instant, The Avenger got a burning shred between his teeth.

No fingers could have gotten a grip on the tiny stub, but teeth could. He pulled it out. There was a terrible fraction of a second when the three waited helplessly on the chance that one spark had gotten through.

Then silence. Harmless silence. The thick, thudding concussion of their own pulses throbbed in their ears.

"*Whew!*" gasped Smitty.

"Oh, b-boy!" Cole said weakly. He leaned against the wall and was not ashamed of his trembling knees.

It had been a second and a half to remember.

Almost equally memorable was the sight of The Avenger, now. Dick Benson had had that thing in such a position that his head would have been blown off as cleanly as an executioner's ax could remove it—if he hadn't caught the fuse. Now, he was calmly examining the instrument of death, and neither in chill, pale eyes nor masklike face could a spark of emotion be seen.

The little bomb was an ordinary beer can filled with powder with the crimped cover put back on and a fuse leading through a hole in the cover. Crude and simple, but if it had gone off there wouldn't have been enough pieces of the three men left to fill a bucket.

At the window, down and outside, clockworks were screwed, which had opened the sash and tipped up the chute. A cheap cigarette lighter had flared with the upswing to light the fuse.

But The Avenger didn't bother for long with the details of the bomb. He set the can carefully on the floor, motioned for Smitty and Cole to wait there, then went down to the vestibule again.

When he came back, he said evenly: "A simple but effective trick. Someone took the Amos Beaker card and put it into the plate of a vacant apartment. This apartment. The card came from the slot belonging to an apartment almost directly under this. A fresh scratch from a knife point, made when the card was removed, gives it away."

They followed his lead, down the stairs, and to the same part of the building. Again, The Avenger listened; again he shook his head as he heard nothing; again he opened a door and the three stepped cautiously in.

Smitty's breath whooshed out. They stared.

This apartment was not vacant! There were four men in it, in the living room. And yet, in a sense, it was vacant because there was no life in it.

The four men were dead!

They lay scattered in the room. One had a broken nose; one had wispy gray hair; one was tall and thin; and one had a babyish face that was gray, now, instead of pink. Beak Nailen and his gang.

The laughing killers had been here first, and none of Beak's unholy crew would ever talk.

The place was further disturbed. It looked as if a cyclone had hit it; looked, in a word, as a place looks when a ruthless and frantic search for something has been made.

"They sure wanted that formula Beak took from Brown's safe," Smitty said. "Look. These guys have been clubbed, stabbed and strangled. No noise like gunshots. That's why no one in the building here seems disturbed."

Benson only nodded. He stepped to the window. There were screw holes outside.

"Nailen is the twisted one responsible for the clock and bomb contrivance," he said. "If the police caught up to them here, the bomb was to kill the lot of them and make a getaway possible. The men who came here simply removed it and put it in that other apartment for our benefit, if we, or *you* happened to catch up to them. I, of course, am supposed still to be in a pump pit with Tate."

Benson put in a call to headquarters. Homicide would want to look this over.

"Think they got that formula?" Cole asked Benson.

"I don't," said The Avenger. "I don't think they were even after it. We'll go back to Bleeker Street. I want a few words with Edna Brown."

CHAPTER XV

The Yacht

The first thing Benson did when they were up in the vast top-floor room at headquarters was phone the hospital where Dillingham Brown lay. He found that Brown was still in a coma, still lying between life and death.

"No chance to get any information there," Wilson observed.

"Nellie, please bring Edna Brown up here," The Avenger said.

The second floor of the building was split into beautifully equipped suites. In one of these was Brown's daughter. She came obediently to the second floor behind Nellie, but a look at the stubborn line around her pretty mouth showed that the obedience was only skin-deep.

"You won't get anywhere pumping me!" that line seemed to say.

"Let me get you a chair," said the susceptible Smitty.

He brought her a big leather easy chair, lifting the ponderous thing as easily as a paper clip, while Nellie glared at him. The pretty ash-blond sat down. Benson stood before her, voice calm and gentle, but pale eyes like diamond drills.

"I believe you know many things that would be helpful to us, Miss Brown," The Avenger began. "You haven't been helpful, so far. I think you should try, now. Your father, in the hospital, surely would want you to aid in tracking down those who nearly killed him."

"I want to help you," said the girl. "I'd like to, very much."

Nellie grimaced. It takes a pretty girl to read through a pretty girl. Nellie heard no conviction in Edna's words.

"Then," said Benson, "tell us what was really in that wall safe. What was it that upset your father so terribly when it was stolen?"

"The . . . the formula for that awful drug," Edna said.

"That surely would be a prize any crook would give his head for," Smitty offered. "Here's a drug that makes a man a laughing robot, immune to pain, ready to go out and murder anyone he's told to—"

"Will you shut up, you big ham!" Nellie said.

Benson went on. "All right, it was the loss of the formula that frightened your father. He came to me and asked for help in recovering it, and he also hired a gang of gunmen to find the robbers and wipe them out."

"Oh, no!" said Edna. "He didn't do that."

"Somebody raided the underworld for hired killers. And then doped them up and sent them out to earn their fees."

"It was the same gang that robbed the safe—"

"Never once, as far as we know, did Nailen or his men laugh. Only the others, the ones who finally killed Nailen and his gang. So if Nailen had the formula, he didn't use it. The others did. But you say they didn't have the formula."

"There was the batch I made up just before I was

kidnapped," Tate cut in. "That would keep them going."

"We encountered the laughing killers *before* you were kidnapped," The Avenger said quietly. He continued to stare at Tate. "You said Brown himself had asked you to steal out of the house with a fresh batch of the pills."

"That's right," said Tate.

"Why?"

"I have no idea," said the young chemist. "I wish Brown was conscious so we could ask him."

Benson turned back to the girl.

"Apparently, when your father came to us for help, you didn't approve," he said.

"I did not," Edna said.

"So, to keep us out of it, you led MacMurdie and me into that trap out at the tip of Long Island."

"No," said Edna. "I mean, I didn't know there'd be such danger—"

"Why did you lead us there if it wasn't to trap us?"

"Please!" gasped Edna, closing her eyes. "I can't tell you any more than I have. I'm . . . afraid to. I don't *dare!*"

She was terrified, for some reason. She shivered on the chair as if some direct death threatened her. The Avenger's immobile lips came as close to a smile as they ever did.

"Very well," he said gently. "I think you're making a mistake in not putting confidence in us, but we'll go ahead and find out for ourselves—"

There was a buzz from The Avenger's desk. He went to it, picked up the phone that had that particular note.

"Benson, please," came a harsh, panting whisper.

"Benson talking."

"Thank heavens you're in!" The words were squeezed out with difficulty. The speaker was obviously in terrible distress of some sort. "This is Xenan."

"Yes?"

"That gang still has me. You've got to help me get away. They're going to kill me! Bring every man you can get. There are at least a dozen of them. Hurry—"

The hoarse, labored words broke off. Then, with appalling clearness: *"Help—"*

After that—silence!

They'd all heard that cry, thin but horrible, through the telephone receiver. Edna, pale as fresh snow, gasped. "What can we do? We've got to do something. But where is he? We don't even know where—"

The Avenger already had the operator. Police and Justice, Inc. could trace any call, any time. The operator gave the phone number and then the location of the instrument just used.

"They've got him on his own yacht," Dick said. "Private dock, Long Island shore."

He went toward the door with that habitual swiftness of movement that had to be seen to be believed.

"Nellie, please stay with Miss Brown. All the rest, come along. You too, Tate."

Nellie started to wail at being left out of the excitement again, but stopped at the look in Benson's eyes. Benson, Smitty, Wilson, Mac, Josh and Tate went to the basement garage and got into the biggest, most heavily armored car in Justice, Inc.'s fleet.

It was well after midnight when the big car purred down a narrow, wooded lane. The smell of the sea was strong.

The Avenger had no running lights on the car. He was driving slowly through what, to the rest, was pitch darkness, but his marvelous eyesight could penetrate the night a little. He suddenly swung to the left. The rest gasped. They thought the car was going to smack against trees, since the lane had been solidly tree-lined, as far as they could tell.

Benson had seen a small bay in the trees and brush, however, and the big car nosed into this. The six men got out, Tate nervous and keeping near the giant Smitty for comfort. Smitty looked very huge and comforting, with trouble around.

The Avenger cut branches and piled them against the back of the car, hiding it from anyone else who might drive down the lane.

"Stay here," he told them in a low tone. "I'll look the boat over and come back."

"And if ye don't?" whispered Mac.

"If I'm not back in twenty minutes, come after me."

"Let me go," Josh protested. The Negro grinned. "I match the night pretty well, you know."

"No. This is my job."

The Avenger was gone, and the rest of them felt like rubbing their eyes. With his uncanny woodcraft, he seemed to have melted into the night—or vanished into thin air—rather than walked away like a normal human.

Dick had stopped about a quarter of a mile from the shore. The shoreline, on the whole, taking all its miles, was crowded along here. But this particular strip was evidently owned entirely by Xenan. There were only woods, for quite a stretch, on either side of the lane.

Benson flitted through the woods like a shadow, keeping wide of the lane. When he got to the water's edge, he was a hundred yards from the dock.

He peered at the big bulk of private wharf and boat with expressionless, deadly eyes. The yacht looked dead and deserted even to The Avenger's telescopic vision, at first. It would have kept on looking that way, to anyone else. But after a moment, he saw a thin crack of light at two of the stern portholes.

Benson stripped to shorts and shirt. With his outer garments went the bulletproof celluglass covering, which rendered him vulnerable. But he had to take that chance. He slipped into the water.

With a slow, smooth side stroke that didn't once break the surface of the water, he slipped to the stern of the yacht. Slowly, he went up the ladder between the side of the stern and the dock and looked about at the dock's level. No figure was in sight in the dimness. If there were guards, they were at the land end, watching for invasion that way.

Benson slid up over the yacht's rail, and instantly sank down in its shadow. There, he wrung out shorts and shirt so they wouldn't drip audibly. Right next to where he crouched was the yacht's phone wire, going over the rail, plugged into the dock connections. It was that wire that had carried Xenan's wild cry for help.

The Avenger started to look around.

The first thing he noticed was that there was no one on deck. Nobody at all. From somewhere near the stern came a faint mumbling of voices; if it hadn't been for that, you'd have sworn the boat was deserted.

The next thing Dick noticed was that the yacht had been stripped as a green field is stripped by locusts. He went into two tiny cabins and looked around with short flashes of his light. They were bedrooms, beautifully decorated. But they were almost empty. Rugs, pictures, and all the furniture that wasn't bolted to the deck, were gone.

The third thing he noticed was that a small high-powered motorboat, hardly larger than a large rowboat, trailed from a stern rope. It was over this that the two faint chinks of light showed. Dick lowered himself into the boat, and pulled himself silently along till he was under the first porthole.

By standing on tiptoe, he could just see in the crack

from which the light came. He saw a solitary figure—Xenan.

The man was in a stout chair, with his arms bound to the chair arms and his legs similarly fastened to the chair legs. He was staring straight ahead, stonily, tensely.

A dozen men were cramped in the room. The air was blue with smoke. Six were playing cards; the rest watched. But no one seemed intent on the game.

One said suddenly, "Damned if I'm going to take any more of that laugh stuff!"

"Why not?" another shrugged. "It hops you up, and you don't hurt if somebody socks you. Good on a job, I'd say."

Benson lowered himself to the boat and crouched there for a moment. Then he slipped over the side again, and went down and down.

When he came up the next time he was clear on the other side, under the dock. And he was minus the undershirt.

He swam back to where his clothes were, put them on, and returned to the sedan.

"All right," he said to the rest.

And he led the way to the dock, keeping to the lane this time.

CHAPTER XVI

Captive Turns Captor

It was The Avenger who saw the darker shadow in the clump of shadows next to some bushes near the dock. He held up his hand. The rest stopped. He went on, circling around the bushes.

The man who was crouching near the shrubbery was staring up the lane. He looked very much on guard, as if he'd heard the approaching party. He had a submachine gun over his knees, and his hands were tight on it.

Probably, he never knew what hit him.

Like a gray ghost, The Avenger came up behind him. One sinewy hand clapped over the man's mouth. The other pressed the great nerve center near the base of the skull.

The man struggled hysterically but was held like a child in Benson's grip. In a moment, he was still. The Avenger took a silk line from his pocket, hardly larger than fishing line, and bound him. He gagged him with a handkerchief, then went on.

They found no more guards. They stole silently onto the dock in the shadow of Xenan's yacht and, in another moment, were aboard. The only slight noise made by any of them was made by Tate. He wasn't trained to move silently.

There was a hatch cover on the foredeck. Benson motioned the others to wait. They sank in shadow, and The Avenger lifted the cover and lowered himself into the small hold of the yacht.

Even his eyes couldn't see in the darkness down there; but he could feel around, and he was familiar with boats. He found the fuel tanks. One was empty. The other, he found by tapping softly, was less than half full. There was gas enough to run a boat this size about thirty or forty miles. No more.

He nodded and came back up, eyes like chips of polar ice. He rejoined the others and led the way toward the stern. There was still a faint sound of voices from the cabin where he'd seen the men playing cards. Benson stole down the companionway.

There was a fairly heavy bolt on the outside of the cabin door. Benson slid it noiselessly shut and motioned for Smitty to stand guard. Then The Avenger stationed Cole at another door, and Josh in the corridor leading back to the galley.

He stood for a moment in the corridor, colorless eyes flaming thoughtfully. Then he went up on deck again and to the stern.

The small boat still trailed back there. He drew it a bit closer under the overhang of the stern, and reached into an inner pocket. He dropped the object he had taken out. It hit the bottom of the small craft, gave out a glassy tinkle, but that was all.

He went below, rejoined Mac and Tate and went to the door of the second cabin from which light had shown.

He opened the door swiftly, but without sound, and stepped into the cabin.

"Hello, Xenan," he said, his voice as expressionless as his colorless, glacial eyes.

Xenan sat up straight, straining against the ropes that bound him to the heavy chair. He stared at Benson with his mouth open. Then light came to his stony eyes and a long sigh of relief burst from his lips.

"Benson! You don't know how glad—"

"Best keep yer voice down," said Mac.

Xenan nodded and picked it up in a lower tone. "I'm quite sure you've saved my life, Mr. Benson. I was beginning to be afraid even you could never get aboard without being discovered and taken prisoner. Hello, Tate. You came, too! Free me, please, one of you."

"In a moment," Benson said evenly.

Mac stared. It seemed odd that The Avenger should come here to rescue this man and then not immediately untie him. Xenan seemed to find it strange, too. He stared in bewilderment.

"There's no hurry," said The Avenger, in the same unreadable tone. "And I'll admit to a great deal of curiosity concerning one point in this affair. I believe you can clear it up for me—"

"What affair?" Xenan cut in, looking perplexed. "It has all been a hopeless jumble to me. Attacks on me and on Brown in my house. And Brown storming in and holding a gun on me; I suppose your man reported that?"

"Yes," said Benson.

Xenan nodded. "Well, as I say, it's all a riddle to me, so I guess I can't answer any important questions. Whatever this thing started out to be, if it was to be anything besides simple robbery of Brown's wall safe, it now seems to have turned into an equally simple plan to hold me for ransom. I have quite a bit of money, and—"

"What was in Brown's safe that was so intensely valuable to you? And to him? That's the one thing that needs clearing up."

"I don't understand," said Xenan. Mac was staring in more surprise than ever. So was Tate.

"I think you do," Benson said.

"Why—you seem to have some kind of suspicion against *me!*" gasped Xenan. "If you wouldn't mind telling me why—"

"Glad to tell you," Benson said. "Brown's safe is robbed —emptied of all contents. Brown is terribly upset by it and terribly anxious to get back something not specified in the loss, something he didn't want to tell the police about. He came to me for help. But Justice, Inc. doesn't mix into straight police business, which this robbery seemed to be. To get me interested in the case, Brown made up a wild tale about a murder drug that sent men, laughing, out to kill whomever they were ordered to kill."

"What do you mean—a wild tale?" Tate cut in. "Those pills of mine—"

"Nitrous oxide, giving the same effect as laughing gas, save that when they are swallowed instead of breathed the conscious will is not affected. Giving a man several of those is slightly more effective than giving him several shots of raw whiskey. But not much. He is insensitive to pain, has increased strength, but is no more murderous than any professional murderer is to begin with."

Benson turned back to the staring Xenan.

"The story of the murder pills sounded impossible when Brown told it. He knew it would. So a man was sent to Mac's drugstore, hopped up on the stuff, to put on an act. That would convince us. He was sent either by Brown or by you, of course."

"*Me?*" Xenan gasped again. "I don't understand. It

is obvious that the men that robbed the safe used the stuff!"

"Beak Nailen was a common crook. Not too smart. He could never get a formula at midnight and know how to make it up, or have it made up, by the next morning. As a matter of fact, he never knew what he had. He burned the formula along with letters and financial papers, without a second thought. Ashes of the burned papers told us precisely what had been taken besides jewels and cash. But, to continue:

"Whatever missing prize was taken from that safe concerns you, too. Brown got in touch with you, acting pretty frantic, I expect, and told you of the robbery and of his decision to get the help of Justice, Inc. It wasn't enough for you. You enlisted a tough crowd of professional gunmen, got a supply of the pills from Tate, and started out on your own hook to locate the thieves."

Xenan was simply staring now, mouth and eyes wide open. Tate spoke up suddenly, humbly:

"I didn't know what he wanted the pills for. He offered a lot of money for them, and I wanted some new laboratory equipment—" His voice trailed off.

"Do you realize what you're saying, Benson?" Xenan said. "You're accusing me of being the leader of the very men who are holding me prisoner here."

"You are," The Avenger said evenly. "I've known that since the fight at your home. You knew of that tunnel from the garage to the cellar, and you didn't warn me of it. That meant you wanted me to be caught, which also meant you were in with the gang. Also—take tonight.

"You phone me wildly for help. You're a prisoner. You know I can trace the call and hurry here. But is it reasonable that a gang of kidnappers would hold you here and let the telephone cable stretch undisturbed, in plain sight, over the yacht rail to the dock connection? Or let you get anywhere near a phone in the first place? This is trap No. 2, that's all, and the fact was quite obvious."

Xenan's open jaw clicked shut, and there was suddenly a baleful sheen in his prominent eyes.

"Your gang of laughing murderers—given the pills to keep up the play acting about the formula—had orders not to kill us till we, or they, had found out who robbed the safe. We might be valuable. Then your crew found out it was Nailen, killed the whole mob, and then discovered that Nailen didn't have what you wanted so badly, after all. So, from then on, the orders *were* to kill us, before we found out too much."

"You devil!" said Xenan.

"If you didn't want things to be brought to light," Benson said evenly, "you shouldn't have gotten us into the case."

"I didn't want to," Xenan spat out. "It was Brown's idea. I couldn't keep him from it. All I could do was play along with him."

The suave rich man was a different individual, now. The prominent jaw stuck out at a vicious angle. The ruthless lips and nose were like something chiseled out of stone. He looked openly as what he really was—a dangerous, nerveless, lawless killer.

"You want to know what was in the safe. All right, damn you, I'll tell you. Much good it will do you—in a few minutes.

"Brown and I were partners years ago. We handled many trust funds, among other things. The funds were lying around idle, doing no one any good. I used some of the securities as collateral for loans, and with the loans I played the market and speculated in other ways. I made money—a lot of money. I put the trust funds back. Do you see anything wrong with that? No! But Brown thought it was wrong.

"He found out the accounts had been falsified. At first, he was going to turn me in—his own partner—and put me behind bars! Then I said I'd write a confession, taking sole responsibility, if he'd let me off. That would clear him if accountants ever found the falsifications as he himself had found them."

"So it was that old confession that was in the safe," said The Avenger, eyes like ice under a polar moon.

"Yes. You see why I wanted it so badly. And you see why Brown couldn't tell the police—or you, for that matter. He was legally implicated, even if not morally."

"I see. You wanted it so badly that several men have been killed at your order." Baleful as they were, Xenan's eyes dropped a little before The Avenger's icy stare. "This seems to clear up Miss Brown's part, too," Benson said. "She knew about the confession; that's plain from her actions. She didn't want Justice, Inc. in on the case. She was sure you had had the safe robbed yourself, to get the confession back. Playing one enemy against another, she led us to a lonely spot on Long Island where you had been previously told to come with your gang, isn't that right?"

Xenan shrugged. "She had me come there, all right. Very mysterious about it. I went, with some men, and all I got was a fight with you. But while I was there, I took the girl away to hold as a hostage. Then your man freed her," he added sourly.

MacMurdie began to sweat. He looked at The Avenger.

"Muster Benson, isn't this mon talkin' pretty freely?" he said. "He's not the kind to admit things so easy!"

Xenan grinned icily at the Scot. Benson paid no attention.

"I told Brown his daughter was kidnapped," The Avenger said. "He suspected at once that you had her, though he insisted she was safe. He raced to your house with a gun. Your men captured my man, Josh, and broke in and rescued you. One of them hit Brown too hard. You sent the servants away and faked a trip to Florida, so you could hold him there till he got better. You didn't dare take him to a doctor. Then we came, and you had to take us prisoner and start that act about being snatched by your own men."

"Right," said Xenan, very airy and arrogant about it. Mac perspired more. Something was distinctly off key here.

The Avenger's eyes impaled the man.

"This all makes Brown out an honorable but very foolish man. But *you*—you took his foolish story about the drug, which was only to enlist my aid, and made a murderous, terrible thing of it. Now you're going to pay for it. You'll die a murderer's death."

"No," said Xenan harshly. "I won't."

And he stood up, with his phony bonds falling in loops to the floor.

"You're the one who will pay, for your recklessness in walking into this trap even when you knew it was a trap. And bringing Tate with you. How very convenient."

"Ye skurrlie!" Mac burred. He crouched for a leap at the man. But it was never made.

The cabin door opened abruptly, and a man backed in. He was so big that he had to crouch to get in. It was Smitty, facing something in the corridor, and holding his hands carefully up.

Following him came Josh and Wilson. After them filed a dozen men—the ones from the other cabin—each with a machine gun leveled at the heads of The Avenger's crew.

"If one of them winks an eyelid," said Xenan, "let them all have it."

CHAPTER XVII

The Getaway

They were herded helplessly into a corner—Benson, Tate, Mac, Josh, Wilson, Smitty. It was a roundup of the entire male membership of Justice, Inc., including the leader. There was deadly triumph in the eyes of the men whose guns could have made hash of the lot with the twitch of a dozen trigger fingers.

Xenan strutted to the door like a minor dictator.

"This has been interesting and instructive, Benson," he sneered. "You were curious about what was in the safe. I, too, was curious about just how much you knew. Each of us has satisfied the other's curiosity; so now the play can end."

"There was a concealed door in the corridor," sputtered Wilson. "They got out behind our backs."

Xenan laughed. He went out, leaving Benson and his men to stare at the muzzles of death. In a moment, there was a vibration through the boat that told of its engines being started. Then there was the slight movement of passage through a calm sea, increasing a trifle as the yacht left shore.

Xenan came back. He stood a generous distance from the doorway.

"You know where to take them," he said to the triumphant gunmen.

They herded The Avenger and the rest out of the cabin and down the corridor. It was a good-sized boat. Under the cabins was a hold about five feet deep. This was split into three compartments, watertight. The hull was steel; the bulkheads were steel. The latest unsinkable type of construction.

Crouched down to keep from hitting their heads in the cramped little hold, the beaten members of Justice, Inc. emerged into the rear compartment. The gunmen backed them into the center one, then started them through that.

Benson said suddenly, "Your orders are to shut us up in the bow?"

"Yeah," said one of them.

"I see," The Avenger said calmly. "So that's how Xenan planned to get rid of you."

The man looked startled, then angry and suspicious.

"What do you mean?" he snarled.

"Xenan can't let you live, with what you know," Benson said. "He's wealthy. You'd blackmail him for life."

"*Aww,* cut the comedy," another growled. "Get up in the bow with the others."

All but Benson had stepped back over the combing into the forward compartment, leaving the gunmen in the middle one. Benson stepped back, too, face masklike, eyes unreadable. His calmness, in fact, rather jarred the second speaker.

"What you got in your mind?" he demanded. "What do you mean about Xenan planning to get rid of us?"

"All of us are in the fore compartment," The Avenger

said evenly. "All of you are in the middle compartment. The sea valve is in the stern."

"Hooey!" The man laughed, but it got rather shaky toward the end. "The guy wouldn't have the gall to try—"

There was a slam, heavy but not loud, as if a safe door had shut! The gunmen whirled. Then they began racing back, bent down to clear the steel beams overhead, to the center bulkhead door. All there heard a laugh come faintly through the steel panel. A mocking, inhuman laugh!

"He *did* it!" screamed one of the gunmen. "This guy called the trick. He did it! He's going to sink the lot of us!"

The middle compartment was suddenly an inferno. The men screamed and raved and cursed. They shot at the steel door, pouring lead at it in a clanging avalanche. A useless avalanche! The door began to look like a sieve; but it was still a thing no man could break down. And there was no lock to shoot out: the bulkhead door was fastened with a heavy steel lever that clamped down into place.

Benson calmly closed the heavy steel door of the fore-compartment, locking them off from the crazed gunmen. Each band, one of criminals and one of crime fighters, was locked into its own cubicle.

" 'Tis a lesson that crime does not pay," said Mac, voice almost even. "They'll drown like the rats they are.

"It's a lesson that crime fighting doesn't pay, too," Cole shrugged. "We get the same as they do."

Harry Tate stared with terror-glazed eyes at these men, keeping their composure by sheer iron will. Tate cracked.

"How can you just stand there and talk?" he screamed. "Why don't you do something? Try something?"

He ran to the porthole and battered the glass out. As if that would help. It was barely ten inches in diameter. Nothing bigger than a cat could get through there. He stuck his face next to it and began to shriek into the night, incoherently, insanely.

"Oh, shut up!" said Smitty. "We're miles from shore, by now, and going farther every minute. Nobody can hear you."

Tate shrieked again. Then his head rocked as he received a deliberate, backhanded slap from Mac. That brought him out of it. He cowered on the steel floor, paralyzed with panic but not bursting everybody's eardrums with it.

"Wait a minute," Josh said suddenly, hopefully. "It's clear that Xenan means to run out farther into the ocean, open the sea valve, and sink the boat with all hands. But there are two watertight bulkheads besides the one in which the seacock is set. The ship won't sink with two compartments out of three in working order."

In answer, Mac pointed a bony forefinger. All eyes followed. In a corner of the steel partition between them and the center compartment was a ragged hole a foot square, burned away recently with a torch.

"Our kind friend, Xenan, thought of that," the Scot said. "The water can get into all the compartments."

In the next cubicle there was suddenly a redoubling of insane shouting. And a few seconds after that, water began trickling in through the ragged hole.

"He's opened the sea valve!" screamed Tate. "Plug up the hole! Tell the men next to us to do the same!"

"Sure," Smitty said ironically. "Just hold your hand over it. That'll stop the pressure of a sinking hull as big as this—easy!"

The lights went out.

Smitty growled in a terrible anger. This was sheer, uncalled-for cruelty, for Xenan to throw the master switch and leave them to die in darkness. He could just as easily have left the lights on till the water stopped the engines, which were carrying the boat out to sea with the steering mechanism automatically set for a straight course.

The gunmen were already crazy in the next compartment. They went crazier. It sounded like some of them were trying hastily to learn to pray.

"Hey!" Mac's puzzled voice came abruptly from the corner where the hole had been cut. "The water seems to be slowing down!"

"Quiet!" The Avenger's voice cut like a knife through the darkness. Then he went on in a lower tone: "Don't any of you say a word about that. It might be heard above decks through that open porthole. You understand?"

There was obedient, if bewildered, silence. The ship kept thrumming out to sea. Out, out. And then there was the sound of another motor, smaller, with a higher note than the smooth thunder of the yacht's engines.

"The motorboat!" snapped Wilson. "Xenan's cast off. He's getting away. That fiend! That monster can condemn a boatload of men to certain death and laugh about it!"

Benson went to the shattered porthole and looked out. Several hundred yards off, circling back toward shore, was a blotch in the blackness. It was the small boat, heading for the land some twenty or more miles distant. Did the lone, ruthless figure in it wave once, triumphantly? Too dark to be sure of that.

"He's gotten away!" rasped Wilson. "I think I'd go down contented if only he went with us."

"He hasn't gotten away," Benson said quietly. "And we're not going down. At least I don't think—Mac, is the flow of water still small?"

"Yes," said the Scot, sounding puzzled about it.

"Good. There was just a chance that the vibration of the motors would shake it out— Now that Xenan is off the boat with no chance to overhear and correct it, I can tell you. The sea valve is plugged. We won't sink."

"What?"

They snapped questions at him. His calm voice came back in the darkness.

"I came out here pretty sure it was a trap. I went ahead to look the boat over and see what kind of a trap. The boat was stripped of everything valuable. There was a small boat in which a man could escape. There was just enough fuel to drive the yacht a way out to sea. It was plain as print: Xenan meant to scuttle it, with us on board, and get away in the small boat. The remedy was easy, too. I dived under the hull, located the vent to the sea valve, and stuffed my undershirt into it as hard and high as I could. When Xenan opened the seacock, water gushed in. But not many seconds after he left, the undershirt was sucked into the valve; it clogged there and reduced the flow to a trickle. We'll float for many hours. But Xenan won't."

His voice became cold, inhuman, like the voice of doom.

"I left Xenan's fate to Xenan, himself. If he relented, showed pity and didn't try to kill us, all would be well. If he went ahead with his plan, he would be the one to die."

Then came the words of fate in the darkness.

"Before we came below, I dropped a vial of concentrated sulphuric acid on the bottom of the small boat."

It was all he had to say; it told the story.

Xenan would have less than ten minutes before the boat sank. Then, twenty miles or so from shore, in water cold enough to paralyze in a few minutes— The finest swimmer on earth couldn't have made it back to land. He'd be in the water now, screaming, floundering, thinking perhaps of the score of men he had coldly sent to *their* deaths.

Smitty drew a deep breath. It was The Avenger's usual justice. Always he placed the criminals he fought, at the end, in a position where they could live if they acted like decent humans, but would die by their own acts if they continued on their murderous course.

Xenan had joined the fateful list of those who had thought they were deadlier than Dick Benson.

Suddenly, a needle point of blue light showed in the darkness. It showed overhead, and in its reflected light they saw the tense face of Benson, eyes slitted against the terrific though tiny glare. Mac knew what was happening.

Mac had once turned out a miniature acetylene torch. It was no bigger than an atomizer. In its glass base was a grayish lump which, when wet a bit with saliva, generated a gas that would burn into steel like any large blowtorch. Dick was cutting through the yacht's deck plates with one of these.

It took a long time before he was done, and once Tate quavered: "Listen!"

They listened.

"I don't hear anything," Mac growled. "What's the matter with ye?"

"I thought I heard Xenan cry out."

They listened again. Nothing.

"Imagination," said Cole. "He'd be too far away to hear, by now."

But his own voice was not quite steady. And when they were able to hoist themselves up on deck through the fresh-cut hole, his sigh of relief was loud.

Benson's face was as masklike as ever, his voice as calm.

"Smitty, go to the wheel and turn us back on our course, to land," he said. "Josh, radio the Long Island police to meet us and pick up a load of murderers. Tell them to send a boat out with fuel; I don't believe we have enough to get us back."

The two went off.

"Won't this gang tell the police about the confession and drag Brown into it after all?" Cole said thoughtfully.

Benson shook his head. The lights flicked on all over as Smitty found the switch.

"Xenan wouldn't have told them the exact nature of the thing he was after," The Avenger said. "That would be leaving himself too wide open to blackmail in case there was a slip-up in his final plan to liquidate them all."

They were safely on their way to shore; they had a boatload of crooks to give to the police; Xenan had unwittingly tried, condemned and executed himself. The case, it seemed, was closed.

But then Tate decided to give vent to outraged feelings.

"You've got a nerve," he shrilled. "You knew this was a trap. Two to one everybody in it would die. Yet you bring me along and make me take the same risk. Me—an innocent man!"

Slowly the deadly, pale eyes turned to meet his own. He repeated, unsteadily, "Me—an innocent m-man—" Then he seemed to run down.

The Avenger held out his hand. "Give me the confession," he said evenly.

"What? What are you talking about?" blustered Tate.

"You have the confession. Brown didn't have it; Beak Nailen didn't have it; I do not have it. There's no one to point to but you—with your frequent access to Brown's safe for your ridiculous formula."

"You're crazy! *Crazy!*"

"You took that confession, days, weeks ago, didn't you? And as luck would have it, the safe was cleaned out and you thought you were forever cleared. Neither Brown nor Xenan knew it, at first. Brown asked you to slip away from the house, afraid under police questioning, or mine, that you'd break and admit the nitrous-oxide pills weren't the real reason for his anxiety. You obligingly went, and Brown suspected nothing. Xenan asked you for more of the mixture. You obligingly made it for him. He seized it and actually held you prisoner. But it was still only to keep you silent; he didn't suspect, even then."

"Y-you're guessing," shrilled Tate. He looked as if he would have turned and fled from the colorless, awful eyes. But there was no place to run to.

"Am I?" said Benson. "Well, Xenan wasn't guessing, at the end. He *knew* you had it. That's why he said, 'How convenient!' when he saw we'd brought you here. He thought he'd kill you with the rest of us and be free of threat for the rest of his life."

"I didn't—I haven't—"

The Avenger's hand was stretched out, waiting. Tate reached into his coat pocket and drew out a heavily taped envelope.

"It was for the good of humanity," he whined. "I wanted a big new laboratory. I didn't want money for myself. And you can't get me for blackmail. I never blackmailed Xenan."

"Only because you didn't have time," said Benson. He put the envelope into his own pocket. "This goes back to Brown. And *you*"—he finished, voice like a whip—"will be careful to walk a very straight path from this night on. You understand?"

He turned and went to the prow. He stood there, looking toward land, like a figurehead of steel. The affair of the laughing killers was over, and justice, he thought, had been done. But there was no satisfaction on his immobile face at a task accomplished. No single accomplishment would ever bring that emotion to his face.

Only the war as a *whole* against the underworld counted with him—not any single battle. He would go on and on in that war, till eventually a bullet or knife blade found his heart. Then, and then only, there might be a look of quiet satisfaction on his face. Then, and then only, there might be relief for his lonely, indomitable soul. Till then, he was less a human than a crime-fighting machine. He was The Avenger!

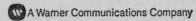

KENNETH ROBESON'S

**DON'T MISS A BOOK IN THIS THRILLING SERIES!
NOW AT YOUR BOOKSTORE, 75¢ EACH:**

If you are unable to obtain these books from your local dealer,
they may be ordered from the publisher.

Please allow 4 weeks for delivery.

WARNER PAPERBACK LIBRARY
P.O. Box 690
New York, N.Y. 10019

Please send me the books I have checked.

I am enclosing payment plus 10¢ per copy to cover postage and
handling. N.Y. State residents add applicable sales tax.

Name ....

Address ....

City .... State .... Zip ....
_____ Please send me your free mail order catalog